The ALCHEMIST'S DAUGHTER

The ALCHEMIST'S DAUGHTER

EILEEN KERNAGHAN

thistledown press

Library and Archives Canada Cataloguing in Publication

Kernaghan, Eileen
        The alchemist's daughter / written by Eileen Kernaghan.

ISBN 1-894345-79-7

        I. Title.

PS8571.E695A64 2004   C813'.54   C2004-904338-2

Cover painting *The Alchemist*, by Lori Koefoed
Author photo: Diane Jarvis Jones

Cover and book design by J. Forrie
Typeset by Thistledown Press
Printed and bound in Canada on acid-free paper

Thistledown Press Ltd.
633 Main Street, Saskatoon, Saskatchewan, S7H 0J8
www.thistledown.sk.ca

 Canada Council
for the Arts
Conseil des Arts
du Canada

 Canadian
Heritage
Patrimoine
canadien

 ARTS BOARD

Thistledown Press gratefully acknowledges the financial assistance of the Canada Council for the Arts, the Saskatchewan Arts Board, and the Government of Canada through the Book Publishing Industry Development Program for its publishing program.

The ALCHEMIST'S DAUGHTER

This one is for Christopher

Charing Cross, 1587

Post mille exactos a partu virginis annos
Et post quingentos rursus ab orbe datos
Octavagesimus octavus mirabilis annus
Ingruet et secum tristitia satis trahet.

Sidonie put down her father's battered copy of Regiomontanus, by all accounts the greatest mathematician-
astronomer of his time. *Octavagesimus octavus mirabilis
annus*: "the extraordinary eighty-eighth year". Regiomontanus spoke of fifteen hundred and eighty-eight years
after Christ's birth — a year when ill-omen was written in
the stars.

There would be eclipses of both sun and moon, while
Saturn, Jupiter and Mars would hang in conjunction with
the moon's house. All this to Regiomontanus, writing in
the previous century, had signalled catastrophe. Other
scholars, examining his findings, could find no error in
them. And then there was the rumoured marble slab,
discovered in the ruins of Glastonbury, on which, inexpli-
cably, Regiomontanus's words were carved. His prophecy
had ended thus: *Cuncta tamen mundi sursum ibunt atque
decrescent/Imperia et luctus undique grandis erit*: "yet will the

EILEEN KERNAGHAN

whole world suffer upheavals, empires will dwindle and everywhere will be great lamentations."

Though her father had spoken often enough of that dire prognostication, until now Sidonie had not thought much about it. With thieves and beggars wandering the roads, talk of conspiracies in every inn and ale-house, and the constant threat of pox and plague, there was reason enough for lamentation in the land. And yet, while wars raged across Europe, England remained withal a blessed haven of peace.

But now this year was halfway done, and 1588 was all too near at hand.

CHAPTER ONE

*Magic has power to experience and fathom things which
are inaccessible to human reason. For magic is a great secret
wisdom, just as reason is a great public folly.*

— Paracelsus

As Sidonie came through the gate she met their maid-of-
all-work Alys stumbling out of the house with her apron
clutched across her face.

"Alys, whatever ails you?"

Alys glared accusingly at Sidonie over her apron hem.

"'Struth, mistress, the reek in that house is more than
any mortal can abide."

"Oh dear," said Sidonie. "Another of Father's experiments?"

"Experiment, indeed. Wizardry, more like. And if he
wants any dinner tonight, he can cook it himself."

In the shuttered laboratory, the usual odours of sulphur
and charred wood, candle-wax and musty books were
overwhelmed by the stench of something moistly rotting.

"Merciful heavens, Father," said Sidonie, clapping her
hand over her nose, "what is making such a stink?"

"Stink, my child?" Her father glanced up abstractedly
from his worktable. "Perhaps it is that basket of herbs that
Alys brought in from the garden."

Sidonie looked over his shoulder at the clutter of flasks and crucibles strewn across the table. She had no trouble finding the source of the smell. "Oh, Father, surely not again?"

Her father gazed sadly at the black, slimy mess clinging to the bottom and sides of an alembic.

"'Tis a great pity, daughter," he said. "This time, I was as close as that to succeeding." He held up his thumb and forefinger, a fraction of an inch apart.

"In playing God, you mean? And which recipe did you follow this time?"

"Why, Paracelsus, to the very letter," said her father. Far from abashed, he seemed pleased at her interest. "One places the seed in a sealed retort, then buries it for forty days in horse dung, along with four magnets in the shape of a cross . . . "

"It is no mystery, then," interrupted Sidonie, "why Alys has fled in disgust, and why the house will need airing for a fortnight."

Simon Quince took off his spectacles, which had rubbed a sore place on his nose, and set them carefully on the table. He peered up at Sidonie. "Why, what has become of Alys?"

"Gone, Father," said Sidonie with exaggerated patience. "Driven away, like all the others."

"These servants," said Simon Quince, "pay them a queen's ransom, and yet they have no steadfastness, no loyalty."

"No," said Sidonie tartly, "but unfortunately they all have noses." Then, curious in spite of herself, she said, "Go on, Father. What happens after forty days?"

"Why then, the homunculus begins to resemble a tiny human form. It breathes and moves, though it is without eyes, and transparent as jelly. Now, one feeds it daily with one's own blood, which carries the *pneuma*, the soul-substance, and keeps it at the steady temperature of a mare's womb. At the end of forty weeks it will have become as a human child in miniature."

"I fear," said Sidonie, eyeing the mess in the retort, "that somewhere you have missed out a step."

"Alas," said Simon Quince, his long, lined scholar's face the picture of melancholy, "when one explores the Secret of All Secrets, there are a great many opportunities for missteps. Still, this is how the Great Work must ever begin, with darkness, dissolution, formlessness. And one day, as God is my witness, I will succeed, and then my name will be spoken in one breath with the names of Paracelsus, and Flamel, and Dr. John Dee."

"And then perchance we will be able to keep a servant," muttered Sidonie, as she threw back the shutters to let in the cool herb-scented summer night.

CHAPTER TWO

Oh Lady Fortune,
Stand you auspicious!
    — William Shakespeare, *The Winter's Tale*

"Daughter!"

Sidonie laid a ribbon in her Euclid to mark the page and gave the soup kettle another stir. "Yes, Father?"

"Did I tell you that Thomas has also abandoned us, hired away by that mountebank Fletcher?"

"That mountebank Fletcher is much in favour at court," Sidonie reminded him.

"Only because Dr. Dee is travelling abroad, and the lords and ladies insist upon their entertainments."

"Then shall I write out an advertisement for a scryer?" Sidonie asked. "You must dictate, I do not know what you wish to say — beyond 'must be willing to work any hour of the day or night, for tuppence a fortnight'."

"Nay, child," said Quince, ignoring this piece of impudence. "I have not time for that. Every vagabond and street juggler in the city will be lined up at our door. I had another thought, just now. Leave off what you're doing, I pray you, and come hear me out."

Reluctantly, Sidonie put down her book. She did not like the sound of this.

As always, when her father seized upon a fresh enthusiasm, his gaunt features softened, became almost boyish. "Sidonie, we've always known that you possess the gift."

"No, Father, I have told you . . . "

Sidonie's hasty protest was cut short.

"I know, my child, you have said that you want nothing to do with sorcery. I do not speak of sorcery, only of scrying. To look into the crystal, to see the future, to discover what is hidden, that is a kind of science, is it not?"

"Not any kind of science I want to practise," Sidonie said. "Father, you know well enough why I will not scry. How can you ask such a thing of me?"

"Because," Simon Quince said gently, "it seems to me wrong, to deny the talents your were born with. It saddens me to see you waste those talents in sweeping and stirring and making beds."

"Then hire another servant," Sidonie said.

"In truth, daughter, we can ill afford to pay a servant, let alone a scryer. And it is the scrying that keeps the wolf from our door. Things were different, when your mother was alive. And clearly you have inherited her gift."

"Her curse, you mean," Sidonie said bitterly.

"If you will. It became her curse. But it does not have to be so. Your mother looked into her mirror, Sidonie — that was her grave error. She looked into her mirror, and saw her own fate. That is more than any of us can bear."

ॐ ॐ ॐ

"Sidonie, child, our fortune is made." Simon Quince came to the doorway of his workroom. There was a folded paper in his hand.

"Indeed?" said Sidonie. She set down her basket of salad herbs. "And how shall this miracle be accomplished?"

"Have I not told you the story of how Queen Elizabeth herself visited Dr. Dee at his house in Mortlake, and asked to see his magic glass?"

"Several times," said Sidonie, only half-listening. She stirred the floor-rushes with the toe of her slipper, sending up a puff of lavender-scented dust. It was past time the rushes were replaced.

"She arrived in a grand procession," continued Simon Quince with practised eloquence, "accompanied by all her Privy Council, and sundry other lords and nobility. But when informed that the house was in mourning, Dr. Dee's wife having died only hours before, Her Majesty declined to enter, and asked instead that Dr. Dee bring out the glass, that she might examine it. Which she did forthwith, to her great contentment and delight."

A dreadful thought occurred to Sidonie. "Father," she said. "Surely you are not suggesting . . . "

"That we invite Queen Elizabeth to come to Charing Cross? Nay, daughter, our house is far too humble to entertain royalty."

Thank heavens for small mercies, thought Sidonie. No matter how grand her father's aspirations, from time to time a modicum of common sense prevailed.

"No, daughter, we are invited to visit the Queen. I have here a letter from Lord Burleigh himself, instructing us to attend upon Her Majesty at Hampton Court."

"This is marvellous strange, Father."

"Marvellous indeed, but hardly strange. With this Spanish trouble brewing, the Queen needs must discover what the future holds — for herself, and for England."

"But she has an astrologer — Dr. Dee."

"Who as you know has gone abroad, leaving Her Majesty with no prognosticator in which she can place her trust. Child, have I not said that I have friends in the highest circles? Friends who will drop a word in the right ear when the time is right?"

"But you have said 'us'."

"I will read the stars for Her Majesty. And you will look into the scrying crystal and see what secrets may be hidden there. Just think, daughter — wax candles again, instead of tallow. A pint of claret with our supper. And you, my clever girl, shall have a velvet hat, and a new gown, with farthingales and furbelows to your heart's content."

"I have a hat," said Sidonie. "And my old gown will do well enough, since I do not go out in society."

"Ah, but you will, daughter," said Simon Quince. "You will come with me to court, and all the young lords will dance attendance on you."

"Aha," said Sidonie, only half teasing. "Now I see which way the wind blows. This is how you will put claret on the table — by marrying me off to an earl. 'Struth, dear Father, you have studied metaphysics too long — you have lost touch with reality."

She imagined how the two of them, dressed like poor artisans, would be received at court — she in her plain woollen kirtle, her father in his shabby russet gown. She had never cared a jot for fashion, never pined as other girls did for silk stockings and doeskin gloves. But neither did she wish to be laughed at. Was her father doomed, as he so often was, to disappointment?

In truth, she too was weary of the lean days when there was no bacon for their pottage, when they had to make do

with pease porridge and oats instead of wheaten bread.
"And if I look into the crystal? Will I see only the fate of
others, not myself?"

"In this crystal, which I have purchased from my
eminent colleague Doctor Forman, you will see the fate of
all of us — the future of England. And that, my daughter,
is the vision that will keep us in luxury in my old age, and
yours."

"But Father — suppose the future of England is disaster
and defeat? What would it benefit the Queen to hear such
tidings?"

Her father had an answer for that, as indeed he had an
answer for most things: "If a man knows that his house is
to catch fire, he may be unable to prevent the fire, for that
is preordained. But still he can try to quench the flames;
or he can choose to gather up his possessions, and go with
his wife and children to an inn, and so survive."

And Sidonie argued in her turn: "But Father, suppose
it is not the fire, but the man's death, and the death of his
family, that is pre-ordained?" It was a conundrum that
made her head hurt, for surely it had no easy answer.

She realized that her father was no longer paying
attention. Quill in hand, he was composing his reply to
Lord Burleigh's letter. With a sigh Sidonie picked up her
Euclid, taking refuge in his reassuring certainties.

CHAPTER THREE

A power I have, but of what strength and nature
I am not yet instructed.
— William Shakespeare, *Measure for Measure*

The scrying stone was a sphere of polished crystal that sat comfortably in the palm of Sidonie's hand. When she held it up before the fire, it blazed with reflected light.

"Hold it away from the hearth," her father said. "Take it into the shadows and look into it by candlelight. Gaze long, and make your mind clear and empty as the summer sky."

She stared obediently, and after a while she felt her eyelids droop, as though sleep were overtaking her. The focus of her eyes changed, her gaze narrowing till it fixed upon a single point of light within the crystal, while everything at the edge of vision blurred. Now she could see yellowish cloud-tatters swirling within the glass, and through them, as through sea-mist, a clustering of tall attenuated shapes. They might have been flagpoles, the bare trunks of winter trees, the lances of an ancient army — or a forest of masts.

In that warm room, a sudden chill seized her. She turned, held the scrying stone before the fire; saw the shapes, whatever they might be, vanish in a blaze of orange light. She set the globe down on the table, resting it carefully against a book.

"What have you seen, daughter?" Her father's voice was sharp with tension.

If you see disaster in the crystal, and you speak your vision aloud, Sidonie wondered, *does it then come true?* "Nothing," she said. "I saw nothing, Father. Only light reflected in the glass."

Chapter Four

Oh Goddess heavenly bright,
Mirror of grace and Majesty divine,
Great Lady of the greatest Isle, whose light
Like Phoebus lamp throughout the world doth shine . . .
       — Edmund Spenser, *Faerie Queene*

On a bright August morning Sidonie set out with her father for Hampton Court. "I have heard," said Sidonie, "that the Queen throws her shoes — or worse still, her wine goblets — at servants who displease her." Holding up the hem of her best skirt with both hands, she picked her way around a heap of refuse.

"And at the gentlemen of the court, as well," said her father.

"Suppose she does not like my foretelling. I should not like the Queen to throw her shoes at me."

"Tush, child," said Simon Quince. "Queen Elizabeth has not sent for you to tell her fairy tales. She is by all accounts a woman of great courage and good sense, and able to look her fortune in the eye. All you must do, is tell her honestly and plainly what you see."

They walked past Queen Eleanour's Cross and down to the river-stairs. A wherry was waiting to take them from Charing Cross upriver to Hampton Court. The boatman, who wore the Queen's scarlet livery, helped Sidonie step from the landing with as much courtesy as if she had been a lady of the court. The sky was a cloudless blue, and everywhere on the river there were flocks of swans. The incoming tide sped them upstream past Westminster Abbey, past the vast sprawl of Whitehall with its stately gardens, past Lambeth Palace on the southern bank, past the fields of Chelsea, till they came in sight of the carved red chimneys rising above the square battlements of Hampton Court.

At the water-gate another scarlet-liveried servant led them up the river-stairs, through arbours and alleys, sheltered galleries, and gardens ablaze with summer blooms. Immaculate beds of roses, sweet William and gillyflowers were edged with railings striped in the Tudor colours of white and green. Banks of rosemary scented the air, and everywhere the Queen's heraldic beasts glowered down at Sidonie from their pillars of stone.

The brick walls of Hampton Court Palace, rising before them, were deep crimson where the sunlight struck them, plum-coloured in shadow, patterned with chequered lines of burnt-black. Sidonie craned her neck this way and that, gazing at turrets and gilded pinnacles, mullioned windows, embrasured parapets. Gargoyles crouched on every gable, and wherever she looked, there were more heraldic beasts: lions, greyhounds, dragons, panthers, leopards, antelope.

They followed the Queen's man across the stone bridge over the moat, and went under the arch of a great gateway flanked by busts of Roman Emperors. Within was a courtyard, and then a second gateway — Anne Boleyn's, said Sidonie's father, pointing to that ill-fated lady's gilded coat of arms.

"Look there," said Simon Quince, as they came into the next court. "There is a wonder to behold, daughter." Sidonie tilted back her head to look up at the famous Astronomical Clock.

"There in the centre is the earth, and on the large pointer is the sun. With those three copper dials the clock indicates the hour, the sign of zodiac, the month, the day of the month, the number of days since the year began, and towards the centre the phases of the moon, so you can predict the tides."

"But," said Sidonie, hoping to forestall what threatened to become a lecture, "according to Copernicus, the earth is not at the centre, the sun is. The earth goes round the sun, not the sun round the earth."

"But the clock was made before Copernicus's time," her father said, in a tone that discouraged further discussion.

The servant led them up a flight of stone steps into the Great Hall, where they were met by a gentleman of the court in black velvet and a gold chain of office. Sidonie trailed behind the others, lingering to examine the curious assortment of furniture and objects in the room — royal portraits, paintings of battles, a history of Christ's passion carved in mother-of-pearl; and tapestries portraying black-skinned folk on elephants in what Sidonie thought must be the Land of Barbarie. There were, besides, an array of elaborate looking-glasses; musical instruments of various sorts; and royal beds, piled high with gold and silver cushions and ermine-lined counterpanes. In these beds, the courtier told them, kings had been born and queens had died.

They proceeded through more corridors and galleries, till they came to a chamber that was all a-dazzle with light and colour, like a vision of heaven. Sidonie's nervous glance took in, all in a rush, the gilded and painted ceiling; the walls, panelled in gold and silver and hung with silken tapestries; and the royal arms emblazoned on a crimson hanging, with an enormous diamond glittering at their centre.

In the chair of state beneath a canopy studded with pearls and precious stones sat Elizabeth herself — looking, thought Sidonie in the first thrill of recognition, more like a gorgeous icon than any woman of flesh and blood. The Queen's gown was white taffeta lined with crimson silk, and covered with rubies and pearls. Over it she wore a silver shawl, loose-woven and delicate as gossamer, that hung to the hem of her skirt. Beneath her jewel-ornamented red wig her high smooth brow and delicate oval face were white as alabaster — their flawless pallor preserved, so Sidonie had heard, with a lotion of egg white and alum and white poppy seeds. Still, it was the face of a woman in her fifties, and in that unforgiving blaze of light, a fine tracery of wrinkles showed beneath the alabaster mask. The eyes, for all their fierce intelligence, looked tired and a little sunken, as though the Queen had not slept well.

Fire and quicksilver, thought Sidonie, gazing at the garments of snow and crimson, the pearls and rubies, the moon-white face beneath its crown of dark-red hair. Sidonie was her father's daughter, and she knew the language of alchemy well. *Rubedo* and *albedo.* Lion and unicorn. The mystical union of male and female, spirit and soul.

I must remember everything, thought Sidonie. *I must fix every detail in my mind — the jewels, the tapestries, the damascene carpets, the harp of glass and unicorn's horn and all the rare and curious objects that stand about the room — so one day I can tell my children how I met the greatest lady in Christendom.* But there was too much dazzle, too much glitter. She felt light headed with the splendour of it all.

"Your Majesty," she murmured, sinking into a much-rehearsed curtsy. She was barely conscious of her father's presence as he made his own obeisance. The Queen's gaze, piercing as a hawk's, was intent on Sidonie; it was as though they were alone in the room.

"They call this chamber 'Paradise' said the Queen without preamble. "It seemed to me that it was a good place for prognostication. It has a certain magic about it, does it not — what say you, Sidonie Quince?"

"Indeed it does, Your Majesty." To her dismay, Sidonie felt herself wobbling a little as she stood up.

"You're a good deal younger than John Dee," observed the Queen. "And safe to say, a good deal prettier. But can you scry as well as he?"

"I will do my best, Your Majesty."

"Show me."

Sidonie took the crystal from its velvet pouch, removed its muslin wrapping. Cradled in her palm, it seemed to gather into itself all the radiance of the jewelled and gilded room. Sidonie let her breath slow, willed her pounding heart to a quieter rhythm. *The Queen needs must discover what the future holds,* her father had said. *For England — and for herself.* There were no shadows in this room to obscure the vision in the glass; the images of clustered spars sprang forth as vivid and as detailed as figures on a tapestry.

But behind those sharper images lay something else: a vague, rounded shape half-glimpsed through curdled mist in the crystal's depths. More sensed than seen, it made

Sidonie's throat tighten with an inexplicable dread. She turned the glass this way and that, trying to make the elusive shape come clear, but almost at once the mist closed over it.

Sidonie drew a long breath. Looking away, finally, she picked up the piece of muslin and carefully wrapped it around the glass.

"Yes? Yes?" The Queen's voice was edged with impatience. "What is it you see?"

"I see what could be church-spires, Your Majesty. Or trees. Or flagpoles, perhaps?" Her glance fell away.

"Could be . . . could be . . . " the Queen said sharply. "Why do you fear to tell me what you see, Sidonie Quince?"

"Because I fear it bodes ill for yourself and for England, Ma'am."

"What I ask most of my subjects is to be honest. You do me no service at all, to tell me only what you imagine I wish to hear. Whatever you say to me now, Sidonie, will be privy to the two of us. Do you understand?"

Sidonie looked up and met that level gold-brown gaze. "I do, Your Majesty."

"Dr. Quince, will you be so kind as to wait without?"

Sidonie's father, looking slightly taken aback, retreated to the corridor.

"So then, Sidonie Quince. What see you in the crystal?"

Sidonie swallowed hard. "Masts, Your Majesty. The masts of a great many warships, advancing on the coast of England."

"Ah," said the Queen, without surprise. "And are they flying the Spanish flag?"

"That may be, Your Majesty. I cannot make out the colours." *Neither the colours*, Sidonie thought, *nor the phantom shape that lies behind them.* Of that mystery, she was not yet ready to speak.

"No matter," said the Queen. She spoke with weary resignation. "You have scried well, Sidonie Quince. If Dr. Dee persists in travelling abroad, I may need your services again. But leave me now — my steward will have a purse for you."

ॐ ॐ ॐ

"Master Quince, Mistress Sidonie, may I detain you a moment?"

Sidonie looked up in surprise at the tall gentleman who waited in the Long Gallery. He wore a cameo of the Queen's head on a heavy chain around his neck and was clearly a person of authority.

"If you would be so kind as to step this way . . . " and with a courtier's easy gallantry he waved them into a small presence chamber off the gallery.

"Lord Burleigh, Sir Francis, let me present the Queen's new prognosticator, Mistress Quince, and her father, Dr. Quince."

Sidonie collected her wits enough to curtsy. Who would have imagined that all in one hour plain Sidonie Quince would meet the Queen of England, and two of the most powerful men in the kingdom?

She knew them well enough by reputation. Even in the Quince's quiet village, folk kept a keen eye on doings at court. The kindlier looking of the two was Sir William Cecil, now Lord Burleigh, Lord Treasurer of England. And the other, with the cold eyes and humourless mouth, was Sir Francis Walsingham, Secretary of State and the Queen's spymaster — master too, by all accounts, of subtlety and subterfuge.

"Do you understand why you are here?" asked Walsingham, with an abruptness that startled Sidonie and clearly flustered Simon Quince.

"Why, to advise Her Majesty of what may lie in store for her, and for England," her father said.

"It needs no clairvoyance," Walsingham told him, "to know that what lies in store for all of us is the Spanish fleet. One of our shipmasters has reported seeing with his own eyes twenty-seven galleons in Lisbon harbour —'floating fortresses', he called them."

"And," said Lord Burleigh, with a hint of malice, "so annoyed was the Queen that she threw her slipper straight in Sir Francis's face."

Sidonie hazarded a sly glance at her father.

"Then with respect, Sir Francis," said Simon Quince, carefully ignoring that I-told-you-so look, "if not for my daughter's gift of sight, why have you summoned us?"

"Not so much for her occult powers," Walsingham told him, "as for her powers of persuasion. The Queen remains insensible of the grave dangers that surround her. I give away no secrets, when I say that she refuses an armed bodyguard, in spite of repeated threats to her person."

"Moreover, the Queen abhors the idea of war," said Burleigh, "and she will not accept the fact that war with Spain is inevitable. She has agreed to lend aid to the Netherlanders to hold back the Spanish; but as you may know, when the Prince of Orange asked her to accept sovereignty of the Netherlands she refused, because it would mean an open declaration of war with Spain."

Sidonie silently added something that Lord Burleigh had left unsaid. *And she was reluctant to sign the death warrant for the Scottish Queen, who openly conspired with Spain against her.*

"Perhaps," said Burleigh, "Her Majesty will believe what your daughter scries in the crystal, though she will not believe what her advisors tell her . . . "

"Which," cut in Walsingham, "brings us to the second reason for this meeting. What my Lord Burleigh has not mentioned, is that going to war costs an inordinate amount of money. On everything I am about to say now, you must swear to keep silent, on pain of both your deaths."

"We swear," replied Simon Quince — seeming not to notice Sidonie's stricken look.

"Then let us come to the point. Sending armed assistance to the Netherlands under Lord Leicester has severely strained our resources; an all-out war with Spain will bleed the treasury dry. England needs more gold, if she is to defend herself against Spain. Leicester's men are starving, yet the Queen is loathe to take bread from the mouths of English children, even in so necessary a cause. We have given the matter much thought, and it occurs to us there could be another way."

Sidonie turned to her father, saw his face light up with sudden understanding. She held her breath. So much depended on what he said next.

"You understand, my lords, that I have laboured a lifetime to create alchemical gold, and have not yet achieved my goal."

"Yet you believe you are close to achieving it?"

Sidonie's mouth went dry; her heart drummed. *Father, Father, go carefully, this is dangerous ground you tread.* She tried to catch her father's eye, tried by sheer force of will to keep him from uttering the words that might condemn them both. But it was no use. In this, as in every other under-taking, Simon Quince would admit no impediment to success — though that success forever eluded him.

"As close as this, my lord," said Simon Quince, and he held up thumb and index forefinger with a hairsbreadth gap between them.

The words were spoken, there was no way to take them back. Sidonie was filled with a terrible foreboding. She understood too well the message in Walsingham's thin, calculating smile.

ॐ ॐ ॐ

"Father, what have you done? " Sidonie, making supper, sliced angrily through a turnip. "You are no closer to turning base metal into gold, than you were when you began."

"Daughter, how can you say that, when every failed experiment takes me closer to success? It is only lack of money that has held me back — money to buy new flasks and retorts, to afford the purest materials and the best grade of charcoal for my furnace. Now I will have the finest equipment that the Queen's money will buy, and I will return her investment a thousand fold."

"And if you do not succeed, Father? You would not be the first alchemist hanged, for promises he could not keep."

"Frauds and charlatans have been hanged, Sidonie, not honest men of science."

How simple he was, for all his arcane knowledge; how childlike in his faith — in himself, and in the world. At times Sidonie felt that he was the child, and she the adult, for she alone in their household had some sense of how truly dangerous the world was, how the smallest of misjudgments, the wrong words overheard, the wrong company kept, could send an honest man or woman to Bridewell prison, or the Tower, according to their station in life.

"Father, can you not see it was all a ruse? The Queen needs no scrying glass to tell her what Spain intends."

"Not a ruse, daughter — a test of your skill, and of your honesty. When next you look into the glass, she will pay heed to what you see there."

"That may be so, but what of Walsingham? He is devious, Father. He says that he wishes you to make gold, and yet he has no faith in the occult arts."

"Because," said Simon Quince, "he recognizes that alchemy is not magic, but science."

Sidonie knew from long experience that it was useless to argue. "If you say so, Father." She set the pot of turnips on the fire to boil. "It is all too metaphysical for my poor understanding."

So many learned men had striven without success to transmute base metal into nuggets of pure gold. It was not for lack of money, she thought, nor from lack of diligence, but because at the heart of the process there must lie some unknown ingredient, some undiscovered secret. It was said that no one could make gold unless he had an honest and upright soul; that much, surely, Simon Quince possessed. But to discover the hidden key, when so many had failed?

She gave the turnips a stir, and picked up her book.

"What is it you are reading, daughter?"

"Mathematics, Father. Euclid."

"May I see?"

Sidonie held out the open book. She found the pure, abstract world of numbers safe and reassuring. One needed no magical talismans, no esoteric wisdom to unlock its secrets, only the application of a logical and exacting mind. But her father had never truly shared her love of mathematics. Its laws interested him only as a reflection of some vast, mysterious cosmic dance. "It's the new edition," she told him, "with the preface written by Dr. John Dee."

"Indeed!" At the mention of Dee's name, she had her father's full attention. "And how well are you able to follow it, my child?"

"Not easily," she admitted, "but I mean to study it until I master it."

"How like your mother you are," said Quince. "She would never leave off any task until she had finished it, whether it was darning a stocking or copying out some antique parchment . . . Now you must help me, Sidonie, in this most difficult of all tasks that lies before me."

CHAPTER FIVE

. . . gardens . . . furnished with many rare Simples, do
singularly delight . . .
— John Gerard, *Herball or General Historie of Plantes*

The summer morning was too lovely to bide long indoors.
Sidonie collected her copy of Euclid and settled herself
on a bench under the apple tree. The air was fragrant with
rosemary, the marigolds in bloom, the larkspurs and holly-
hocks making a fine show against the sun-drenched brick
wall. Then Mistress Platt, the tailor's wife, shattered
Sidonie's contemplative mood, peering over the garden
gate to remark, "Your beds want weeding, my girl."

"Our servant has left," muttered Sidonie, caught betwixt
annoyance and guilt.

"And have you not a strong young back and a pair of
hands at the end of your arms?" asked Mistress Platt. "My
advice is to take your nose out of that book, and tend to
what needs doing. It quite escapes me, how you young
flibbertigibbets ever hope to get husbands."

"And what business is it of yours, you meddlesome old
biddy?" inquired Sidonie, not quite audibly, as Mrs. Platt
continued down the lane. But it was true the garden
needed her attention. Quickgrass and chickweed were
invading the once tidy plots of salad herbs. Green scum

covered the fishpond, from which the fish had long since vanished, Bindweed was strangling the gooseberry bushes and the roses were sadly in need of pruning. Sighing, she put aside her book and went to the garden shed to fetch a hoe.

Whatever else might suffer from neglect, Sidonie meant to keep the physic garden in good order, for it had been her mother's special pride. The fennel and camomile, the sweet basil and valerian and feverfew, still grew as vigorously as when her mother was alive to tend them. But the deadly witch-herbs — nightshade, wolfsbane, monkshood — no longer grew in Sidonie's garden. The week that her mother died, Sidonie had torn them out by the roots and burned them.

Still half in a temper, she slashed at a clump of buttercups that had sprung up where they had no business to be.

"Sidonie, Sidonie, what has prompted this unseemly attack on those defenceless posies?"

Kit Aubrey, the apothecary's son, sat grinning on the low wall that separated their two cottages.

"Better the buttercups," said Sidonie, "than Mistress Platt."

"Ah," said Kit. "And what has the goodwife said to so enrage you?"

"Only that I am a flibbertigibbet who will never find a husband."

"And were you looking for one?" asked Kit, all innocence.

"Most certainly not. But she has no right to say such things."

"Indeed. But I would marry you in a minute . . . "

Sidonie looked up in alarm.

" . . . if for your dowry you would offer me your father's library."

Sidonie laughed. "And what have you come to borrow? I will go and ask him."

"Mr. Turner's *Herbal*, if I may. I have a mind to go botanizing on the heath."

ॐ ॐ ॐ

Sidonie much preferred the smells of old calfskin and ancient dust in her father's library to the chemical stink of the workroom.

In the tall oak cases that lined the walls, old oft-consulted books — Agrippa's *Three Books on Occult Philosophy*, Roger Bacon's *Mirror of Alchymy*, works by Paracelsus, Albert Magnus and Nicolas Flamel, shared the crowded shelves with newer volumes, some with pages still uncut. More books — the latest acquisitions — were stacked on tables, benches or the floor. Kit read off some of the titles, his glance skimming the shelves and lighting now and again on some rare edition.

"Those cannot leave the library," cautioned Sidonie. "Nor can I take them down from the shelf, save with Father's special permission."

"And does he give you that permission?"

"For most. Not all. He says there are some that must never be opened, for fear of unleashing magical forces that even he can not control."

Kit lifted an eyebrow. "Even he?"

Sidonie smiled at that. "So he says. You know my father, Kit — apprentice of all magics . . . "

" . . . And master of none?"

"Just so," said Sidonie, thinking ruefully of the homunculus, and all the failed experiments that had come before. "But the herbals — you may help yourself to any of those, and keep them as long as need be. You will be wanting to take them with you to the university, I expect."

"Nay, Sidonie, I have not told you — I will not be going to the university after all."

"But Kit, you were to study medicine, you were meant to go to Oxford and become a physician."

"Too far away, alas, and much too costly. It is seven years to a Master's degree before one can begin the study of medicine. Remember, my father is only a poor apothecary, and the business has not prospered these last few years. I am not the son of a Lord of Parliament, who can pay a few shillings to shorten his term of study. "

"There are fellowships . . . "

"And nowadays even those go by favour. I dare say I could attend the Inns of Court, and learn about quiddits and quillets and recognizances, whatever those might be. But the law is a narrow kind of study. Better to be of some actual use to people."

He ran his hand lightly over the shelf of natural philosophy, pulled down Turner's *Herbal,* and held it up so that Sidonie could see the spine. "No, it is decided — I will follow my father's craft. Better that than becoming a barber-surgeon or a pettifogging lawyer. I will study the proper use of medicinal herbs, and as for the rest, I can read Hippocrates and Aristotle as well here as at Oxford."

"I wish I could attend the university," Sidonie said. "But I am doubly disappointed, being not only poor but a woman."

"And what would you study, Sidonie, had you been born a rich man's son?"

"Why mathematics, of course."

"A gentleman's subject, if ever there was one."

"That may be. But the Queen knows mathematics."

"And I'll wager you know more now, than those rich men's sons at Oxford, who waste their all time in drinking and dicing."

"I would not go to Oxford," Sidonie said. "I would travel abroad, to one of the great universities like Padua. Or perhaps if there were still nunneries in England, I would hide myself away from the world, devoting my life to scholarly pursuits."

Kit gave her a sharp look. "Promise me that you will not speak of nunneries where there is anyone to hear."

"I know," sighed Sidonie. "For such sympathies, I could lose my head. And besides, I doubt I would find a nun's life congenial. But all the same . . . "

Kit, who had been thumbing through another herbal, looked up inquiringly. "All the same?"

"To be safe within stone walls, dedicated to study and the service of God, not having to see what is meant to be hidden . . . "

"For that you would rise at three o' the clock, and kneel on cold stone floors."

"Yes," said Sidonie, soberly. "I do believe I would."

CHAPTER SIX

That you should hatch gold in a furnace, sir,
As they do eggs, in Egypt!

    — Ben Jonson, *The Alchemist*

Sidonie came home from the market one late August morning to the smell of smouldering charcoal. Glancing into the laboratory, she saw her father at his work table, setting out an array of flasks and retorts. Hearing her step, he called out, "Sidonie, come and look, I am about to begin the process." She set down her basket and went into the workroom. Her father's face was flushed and damp from the heat of the crucible, his eyes alight with excitement.

He said, without preamble, "Have I explained to you, Sidonie, how all things in nature strive to perfect themselves?"

"More than once," said Sidonie. She settled herself on a bench, preparing to be lectured.

"You understand then, that as the worm becomes a butterfly, as the egg becomes a chicken, so does base metal strive to become gold. Our task is to assist the metal in its metamorphosis from the imperfect to the perfect."

"Why, then," asked Sidonie, who was in a contrary mood, "does the soup kettle insist on remaining pot-metal, when it could turn itself to gold and have a whole new career at court?"

"We speak of the Great Work, daughter. It is no subject for levity." Simon Quince's voice was gently reproving. Still, he chose to reply as though Sidonie had asked a serious question.

"The difficulty is this — that in order to accomplish the transmutation, an agent of change, an elixir, is needed. When this elixir touches any substance, no matter how base, it permeates it, and transforms it into its own golden nature."

"And what is this magical elixir?"

"Ah, but that is the great mystery, daughter. It is said to be made of fire and water; it is a stone but not a stone; it is unknown yet known to everyone; it is worthless and yet valuable beyond price. The alchemist Lully said that with this elixir, he could turn the very seas to gold."

"Then," remarked Sidonie, "the Spanish could walk all the way to Plymouth, to the great confusion of Her Majesty's navy."

She was sorry, as soon as the flippant words were out, but her father seemed not to have heard them.

He said, "I have found, in the writings of the adepts, a formula for producing this elixir. Though the processes are cloaked in symbolism, I have managed to decipher them. Thus it is no longer a matter of trial and error, but a progression of steps one may follow to achieve one's end."

Just what you said about the homunculus, thought Sidonie. But she wisely held her tongue.

"Remember, daughter, these are secrets men have died for. I would not think to share them with any but my own flesh and blood. Do you take my meaning?"

"I do," said Sidonie, chastened.

"So then. One must first reduce one's material to the *prima materia*, the First Matter, which is matter without properties, the possibility of all things. And then by means of many exacting processes, one releases from this First Matter the divine spark, the quintessence, which animates all things. Whoever can free this fifth element from the matter it inhabits, holds in his hands the secret of trans- formation."

"And has anyone succeeded in doing this?" asked Sidonie .

"Why daughter, there have been notable successes. Paracelsus himself possessed the elixir of transmutation. It is said that he heated a pound of mercury, and then dropped into the crucible a few grains of powder, which he called 'the red lion' because of its dark red colour. In half an hour he asked his assistant to look into the crucible and say what he saw there.'I see a yellow substance,' said the assistant. 'It looks like gold'. 'Yes,' said Paracelsus. 'That is what it is supposed to be.'"

"I have heard," said Sidonie, straight-faced, "that breathing mercury fumes can give one peculiar visions."

"That may well be. But let me finish my story. Then Paracelsus said, 'Take this gold and sell it to the goldsmith who lives above the pharmacy.' And the goldsmith attested that it was pure gold, weighing a pound minus half an ounce. There is a rumour also that Dr. Dee and his assistant Edward Kelley have obtained a supply of this same powder; and that with a single grain, no bigger than the finest grain of sand, they turned an ounce of mercury into an ounce of pure gold. Moreover, they cut a piece out of a warming pan, and turned it into silver. Even now they are practising their alchemical arts in the courts of Poland and Bohemia. Can we offer to do less for our own Queen?"

"And what substance do you mean to transmute?"

"Unfortunately, the adepts do not tell us what is to be used for raw material. Some have experimented with grass or mandrake roots, with honey, or wax, or wine, or eggs, or all manner of unlikely materials. None of them had succeeded, as far as I can tell. I have decided to use copper, which has more in common with gold than any of those. See, I am about to begin the work, the black stage, the *nigredo*, by heating the copper with sulphur."

"Then I'd best throw open all the doors and windows," Sidonie sighed, "for whatever else you may produce, we can depend on a terrible stink."

ॐ ॐ ॐ

Sidonie was hanging linen to dry in the garden when she saw the stranger at the gate. She pushed back her hair, lank from the steam of the laundry vat, and hastily tied a kerchief over it.

At first glance she took the tall, stooped figure with its limping gait for some elderly scholar, come to consult her father's library or while away the afternoon in metaphysical discussion. But as she came to greet him, she saw that she had been deceived by the drab black gown and ungainly walk, and in fact the visitor was little older than herself. He was bareheaded, dark-haired, with a narrow, thin-lipped face. His eyes, a pale intense silver-grey, seemed to look straight past her. He said, "I have an appointment with Dr. Quince."

"He is in the library, I believe," said Sidonie, more than a little flustered. "I will show you the way."

41

He followed her inside, with no thanks and no attempt at conversation. His long black sleeves drooped limply, the hem of his gown swept the floor like a seventy-year-old's. *He mistakes me for the serving-woman,* thought Sidonie, and this, together with his odd dress and uncivil manner, disposed her less than kindly towards him.

She showed him into the library, closed the door, and went out to deal with the rest of the laundry.

"Who was it came to see you today?" Sidonie asked her father as they sat down to supper. "I don't believe I recognized him."

"Ah, did I not tell you, daughter?" Simon Quince broke off a generous chunk of yesterday's bread. "I have decided to hire an assistant."

"Father!" Sidonie banged a dish of boiled cabbage down on the table, hard enough to make the ale dance in the beakers.

"My dear?"

"How are we to find the money to feed another mouth, or worse, to pay his wages?"

"Ah, but that is no longer a difficulty, daughter. Remember the funds Her Majesty has advanced me."

"And did you not think, since we are now so rich, that I could have used an assistant? Father, I have been bent over the washing-vat since dawn, because we have no servant, and I believed there was no money to send out the linen."

"You had only to mention it, Sidonie."

"Yes, well," said Sidonie grimly. "There. Now I have mentioned it. And who, may I ask, is this apprentice you have so summarily hired?"

"No apprentice, daughter. A fully qualified assistant. He comes with the highest credentials, having worked abroad with alchemists in the courts of . . . "

"And have you proof of that," interrupted Sidonie, "or merely his word?"

"My dear, have you so little faith in my judgment? He supplied letters of reference, needless to say."

"As did your last assistant but one," Sidonie reminded him caustically. "The one who nearly set fire to the house."

Simon Quince said with a look of contrition, "Sidonie, I have only two hands, and there are only so many hours in the day. I cannot accomplish this great work by myself."

Sidonie dropped into her chair, put her elbows on the table and her chin in her hands, and gave a sigh of defeat. "Have your assistant, then, Father. Though I mislike the man, for he has a peculiar look about him. And from now on I will send out the linen to be washed."

CHAPTER SEVEN

*The scarlet red colour of the flying lion . . . resembles the
pure and clear scarlet of pomegranate seeds . . . It is like a
lion which devours all the purely metallic nature and trans-
mutes it into its own substance, namely, into pure and true
gold, finer than that from the best mines.*
— Nicholas Flamel, *The Hieroglyphic Figures*

"Kit, he is so foolish, my father — so sure of success, and
so far from succeeding. The fault is mine. I have let him
go on, with one ill-fated experiment after another, doing
nothing to discourage him."

Kit plucked an apple from a low-hanging branch and
tossed it into Sidonie's lap. "What could you have done? It
is hardly a daughter's place, to chide her father for his
faults."

"I should have smashed his flasks and alembics on the
hearthstones," said Sidonie fiercely. "But how could I have
known where his foolishness would lead him?"

"Sidonie, are you so sure he will fail? Have not other
alchemists succeeded?"

"Dr. Dee has succeeded, my father says. And Edward
Kelley, Dee's assistant. But they had a secret elixir, a red
powder which is needed to complete the transformation
from dross to gold."

"Where does one find this elixir?"

"I think you are supposed to make it, but that is the most difficult part of the process. Too difficult for my father, at any rate." She bit absentmindedly into the apple. It was still green, and so sour it made her lips pucker. She grimaced and spat it out.

Kit said, "My father sold a packet of sleeping powder to one of the servants from Whitehall Palace. It is all the talk of the court that Dr. Dee, who is living abroad at Trebonam, turned part of a warming pan into silver, and sent it to the Queen."

Sidonie looked up with sudden interest. "Yes, as proof of his experiments. That is the very warming pan my father talked about. The tale must be true, then."

"If you can believe palace gossip. The Queen must believe it, because they say she has sent a great many letters to Dr. Dee, imploring him to return."

"So he can turn more warming pans into precious metal."

"So it would seem. In any event, there is more to the rumour."

"Kit, do not torment me. Prithee, go on."

"Dee and Kelley are said to have come into possession of a Powder of Projection. This must be the elixir — the red powder — of which your father spoke."

"And where did they find it?"

"Buried in the ruins of Glastonbury Abbey, so the story goes."

"Why ever there?"

"Well, they do say it is the most magical place in England, because Joseph of Arimathea hid the Holy Grail in the Chalice Well."

"Then Kit, I must go to Glastonbury."

Kit stared at her. "What, on the strength of some muddled rumour whispered round the palace?"

"Perhaps the rumour is not muddled. Palace servants overhear a great many secrets, and some of them are true. If my father can make gold for the Queen while Dee and Kelley are tarrying in foreign courts, then his fortune is assured."

"Sidonie, this is utmost folly. I did not imagine you so imprudent."

"What is imprudent," Sidonie said, "is to do nothing, and see my father's head stuck on a pole over Tower Bridge. Kit, if I have any gift at all for seeing what is hidden, then I should use it for my father's sake. I will look into the crystal, and maybe see if this tale of Dee's proves true."

ॐ ॐ ॐ

Sidonie carried the scrying crystal upstairs to her bedchamber, unwrapped it and set it carefully on her table amidst a clutter of papers and books. She drew the curtains over her dormer window to shut out the slanting evening light, pulled up a cushioned bench, sat down, and stared resolutely at the crystal. She could feel her heart beating too quickly, her stomach knotting with apprehension.

If this gift or curse of mine will save my father, she told herself sternly, then I needs must find the courage to use it. Deliberately she slowed her breath, emptied her mind, let her gaze narrow and change its focus.

But how to begin? *Perhaps,* she thought, *if I make a picture in my mind* . . . What had her father called Dr. Dee's red powder, the secret elixir of transformation?

The red lion, he had said. She thought at once of those proud heraldic beasts that guarded Hampton Palace. The picture leaped fully formed into her mind: a dark red lion, the colour of crimson silk, rampant on a field of gold.

Strangely, in spite of her misgivings, the scrying seemed easier this time. The glass cleared almost at once, revealing vivid images in its depths.

She saw, first, an ancient abbey of grey stone, roofless and fallen into ruin, its tall arched doorways open to rain and wind. That vision faded, and now a solitary hill rose sheer from a level plain. Around its steep slopes a spiral path coiled, and its narrow summit was crowned by a broken tower.

And then the light faded from the heart of the crystal, and mist flowed in.

A ruined abbey. A hill crowned by a broken tower. Since King Henry dissolved the monasteries some fifty years before, there were crumbling abbeys the length and breadth of England. How could she be sure that the image she had scried was Glastonbury?

Kit will know, she thought. *The world is not such a mystery to Kit as it is to me.*

Chapter Eight

Thou and I
Have thirty mile to ride yet
By dinnertime.
        — William Shakespeare, *Henry IV, Part I*

"What new plots are afoot, Sidonie, that you send me urgent messages with the bookseller's 'prentice?"

Kit vaulted over the garden wall and flung himself down in the warm shade under the apple tree.

"'Come at once and I will reveal all.' Now there's a communication to set the blood astir."

Sidonie laughed. "I knew that the greater the mystery, the sooner you would arrive. No plots, Kit. A journey. I have made up my mind to go to Glastonbury."

Abruptly, Kit sat up. "What, now?"

"Nay, in a fortnight. This is my one chance, Kit, before the autumn rains make the roads impassable. In mid-month my father goes to London with his new assistant, to visit the bookshops and spend the Queen's money on alchemical supplies. He plans to stay for a week or more with his great-aunt Catherine, who is ailing. Until he returns I will be alone in the house, save for our new maid-of-all-work, and her I will swear to secrecy, on pain of instant dismissal."

"And what part do I play in all this?"

"Why, I would have you come with me." She smiled at his look of consternation. "Kit, you would not have me travel alone? And what else have you to do, now that you have decided against a scholar's life?"

"My father would have a quick answer to that," said Kit.

"But a herbalist can always find an excuse for searching fields and hedgerows, however distant — and is there not special magic in the Glastonbury earth?"

"And you," sighed Kit, "have an answer to everything."

"Then it's decided," Sidonie told him. "You are compiling a new book of medicinal herbs that grow in the Vale of Avalon, and on the slopes of Glastonbury Tor."

"And you?"

"I am your sister, and your assistant," said Sidonie. "In a fortnight, then?"

"And have you a pair of horses hidden somewhere about your cottage, Sidonie? Or do you propose we go by shank's pony?"

"We can go quicker by carrier's cart than on foot. I have made inquiries — there is a carrier returning from London to Salisbury every Monday. In Salisbury we can hire post horses, or walk if we must."

ॐ ॐ ॐ

The morning of their departure Sidonie rose by candle-light, put on an old woollen kirtle, a sensible felt hat with a shady brim, and her stoutest shoes. Fastened to a cord around her waist were her leather purse, a number of small bags filled with useful herbs, her scissors and sewing case, and a clove-studded orange in a pomander ball to ward off plague. The scrying crystal, wrapped in several layers of felted cloth, went into a capcase of her mother's, along with spare petticoat and stockings. She dropped her Euclid into one of her pockets, and gathered together her provisions — a loaf of bread, some cheese and cold bacon, a jug of elderberry wine. Then she threw over her shoulders a well-worn and out-of-fashion cloak from her mother's clothes-chest.

Leaving the servant Emma snoring softly in her curtained alcove, Sidonie tiptoed down the stairs. There was one more task she must attend to. She went into her father's workroom, took a folded paper from her pocket, and laid it on the table with an empty retort for a paper-weight.

"Father," she had written. "I have gone to Glastonbury. Kit is with me, and I will be soon returned." If all went well, she meant to be safe home before Simon Quince left London, and he need never see the message.

She gave a last housewifely glance around, and closed the cottage door quietly behind her. Kit, wearing high boots and a travelling cloak as countrified as her own, was waiting in the garden. Together they set out through the deserted lanes of Charing Cross, past the sleeping cottages, to catch a carrier wagon bound with a consignment of Rhenish wines for a manor house at Salisbury.

ॐ ॐ ॐ

They rattled through the Westminster gate at first light, leaving the Strand and the waking city behind them. The post road to the west was crowded with the carts and wagons of country folk, bound with their produce for the London markets. Before long Sidonie could see, above the roofs of the Abbey and Lambeth Palace, the first thin line of sunrise.

Gazing through the dawn mist at the long rough road that stretched before them, she felt a faint shiver of premonition down her spine.

"Are you cold?" Kit asked solicitously. "Shall I lend you my cloak?"

"I'm not cold," Sidonie told him, "just a little affrighted, of a sudden."

"It's not too late to turn back," Kit said.

She shook her head. "I must finish what I have begun. My father tells me that is a failing I inherited from my mother."

"Not your only failing, I would venture," Kit said, laughing. "What would your father think of this escapade?"

"I suppose he would forbid it. That is, if his mind was not preoccupied with metaphysics." She added, a little wistfully, "My mother would certainly have forbidden it. But then, if my mother were alive, there would be no need to make this journey. She was the only one my father ever listened to, the only one who could laugh at him and make him see his folly."

"How did your mother die, Sidonie? You have never told me."

"No," said Sidonie. "I have never told anyone." A lump had lodged like a stone in her throat. "She went into the garden and gathered monkshood, and made it into a tea, and drank it."

"But why?"

"Kit, we never knew. But I can guess. It was the year of the plague, 1583. I was only thirteen, but I remember how, even so far from the city, we lived in terror. My mother looked into a mirror, and she said she had seen her own death."

"Of plague?"

"That may have been what she saw. We will never know. We escaped the plague, my father and I. But my mother, who often visited the poor and sick of our village, to take them herbs and potions . . . "

"Ah," said Kit. "She might have taken the plague, unwitting . . . "

"And brought it into our house. I think that is what she saw, when she looked into the mirror. And so by taking her own life, she cheated fate."

"Did she cheat fate, I wonder? She died all the same."

"But we lived. She would have counted that a victory, I think."

"Is the future so inalterable, then? Might she not have chosen instead to give up her good works, to bide at home till the danger was past?"

"You did not know my mother, Kit. She could never have turned her back on anyone who needed her."

"And you, Sidonie? Do you believe that what you see in the mirror must be your fate?"

"Have you not observed," Sidonie said, "that I never look in mirrors?"

ॐ ॐ ॐ

All day the carrier's cart lurched and jolted its way past sheep pastures and shorn fields. The hedgerows were a bright tangle of honeysuckle and wild clematis. It had rained in the night, settling the end-of-summer dust, and the air was cool and fragrant. *How beautiful the world is,* thought Sidonie. *How can anyone bear to leave it?* All the same, after a long day of jouncing over ruts and potholes, she felt as though she had been rolled downhill in an empty barrel. Her head ached, her backside was bruised, and she could think of nothing but a soft place to sleep.

"When we reach Silchester," she told Kit, "I will buy you a good supper, and a bed at the inn."

"Have you money enough?" asked Kit. "I had resigned myself to spending the night under a hedge, with the rest of the vagabonds."

"Not I," said Sidonie. "I saved a few shillings from the housekeeping so we should not have to sleep rough."

In growing darkness they rattled over the broken cobbles of a village street. The Red Lion, announced the brightly painted sign at the hostelry's gabled front.

"An omen," Sidonie told Kit, only half in jest. "Now we know we are on the right path."

The inn at Silchester was a humble enough establishment. Still, to Sidonie's discerning eye it seemed clean and properly kept, the rushes on the floors sweet-smelling and the bedrooms freshly aired. For supper there was cold roast mutton, pigeon pies and bread and butter, with currant cake and apple pasties after, and plenty of barley ale.

But as they sat down to eat she whispered to Kit in embarrassment, "The rooms are dearer than I thought. Two would be a great extravagance."

"Then take one for yourself," said Kit obligingly. "A corner of the stable will suit me well enough."

"Fie, Kit," said Sidonie. She spoke with brisk assurance, to cover the awkwardness of the moment. "I have put you to enough discomfort on this journey. We are brother and sister, remember, and I trust you to behave as a brother would. You shall have the featherbed, and I will ask for a pallet on the floor."

"And what brother would ask his sister to sleep on straw while he slumbers on goosedown? Unless — " Kit set down his tankard and added with a teasing grin, "I borrow a sword and we do as Tristan and Iseult."

Sidonie gave him a sharp look. "Enough," she said tartly. "If you imagine I will lie with a sword down the middle of the bed, then you'd best sleep with the horses after all."

ॐ ॐ ॐ

Sidonie drew the bed-curtains, undressed to her smock, blew out the candle, and climbed between clean lavender-scented sheets. She heard a soft thump, and then another, as Kit, in the far corner of the room, drew off his boots. His straw mattress rustled faintly.

For a while she lay in the darkness, listening to the slow, deep sound of Kit's breathing, and taking comfort in his presence. Then she too drifted into sleep, and did not wake till dawn.

CHAPTER NINE

O villany! Ho! let the door be lock'd
— William Shakespeare, *Hamlet*

Emma was scrubbing the hearthstone on her hands and knees. With both Dr. Quince and the young mistress out of the way, what better chance to give the cottage a good turn-out?

Behind her, the front door opened and closed. She reached out for the poker, and scrambling to her feet she turned with it raised to strike. "Oh," she said, letting the poker fall to her side. "It's you. Have you not manners enough to knock?"

"Forgive me if I startled you. The door was unlatched."

"Still no reason to walk in as though you owned the place. And why are you here at all, and not in London?"

"I'll not be staying. There are some papers I've been sent to fetch."

Emma could tell that was all the answer she was likely to get.

CHAPTER TEN

There is on the confines of Britain a certain royal island,
called in the ancient speech Glastonia, marked out by broad
boundaries, girt round with waters rich in fish, and with
still-flowing rivers, fitted for many uses of human indigence,
but dedicated to the most sacred of deities.

— St. Augustine

Late the next day they came to Salisbury. As they crossed
the meadows the sun was just setting behind the slender
spire of the cathedral, and the city was wrapped in a blue
haze of woodsmoke. The cart rattled through quiet streets
past the deserted marketplace and drew up in the
courtyard of an inn.

Settled at last in the inglenook in front of a blazing fire,
Sidonie sipped a beaker of mulled ale and felt herself
slipping into a comfortable half-doze. But just as sleep was
about to overcome her, something — a prickling sense of
unease, the faint weight of curious eyes upon her —
brought her abruptly awake.

"Kit," she whispered. "Pray don't stare — but is someone
watching us?"

Kit turned to her with raised eyebrows, then glanced
covertly round the low-ceilinged, smoky room. "None that
I can see," he said. "Wait now . . . that fellow on the bench

beneath the window, with his nose thrust into his beaker. Methinks just now he was looking this way. What of it, Sidonie?"

She followed Kit's gaze to where a man in nondescript dark garments huddled over his ale, his face in shadow. All she could see was lank black hair falling over narrow black-clad shoulders, and, stretched out under the table, one of his legs in a dusty riding boot.

She shrugged. "Perhaps it was only a fancy of mine. I am weary of travel, and my nerves are all a-jangle. I will be glad to go on foot tomorrow, and walk the aches out of my bones."

ॐ ॐ ॐ

Come dawn they breakfasted on cold game pie and paid the reckoning. Crossing the innyard they came upon a carrier wagon laden with carpets, bolts of cloth and fine bed linens, bound for a gentleman's country house near Wells. "Here's a piece of good fortune," said Kit, after conferring with the driver. "There's space for us in the back of the wagon, and he's travelling straight through till tomorrow morning. We'll save the price of another night at an inn, and from Wells it's an easy day's walk to Glastonbury."

Sidonie looked into her purse and found it was emptying faster than she had hoped. "Then you'd best hire us two places," she said resignedly, fishing out tuppence. She dreaded the thought of a sleepless night in a jolting wagon, wedged in among carpet rolls and packing chests. Still: *'twas you who chose to make this journey, my lass,* she told herself sternly; *now you must needs put on a cheerful face, and make the best of it.*

ॐ ॐ ॐ

At Wells they parted company with the waggoner, and followed a sheep-track that led across the green pasture-lands to Glastonbury.

"There is the Tor," said Kit, pointing to a strange, steep-sided hill that rose like a beacon from the misty fields and osier beds. And Sidonie quickened her pace, her weariness for the moment forgotten. She had seen in vision that mysterious, beckoning shape.

Towards evening they came to the desolate ruins of the Abbey. Standing knee deep in long rank grass, Sidonie gazed silently at the crumbling ivy-covered walls and shattered piers. There was a sick, hollow feeling in her belly. *The holiest place in England,* she thought. *What wickedness can men achieve, and swear it is God's work.*

Kit said, "Is this the place?"

She nodded. "Just as I saw it in the crystal. But Kit, it much troubles me, to see with my own eyes what destruction has been wrought."

"Had you but seen it in its glory," said a quiet voice. Sidonie spun round.

He had crept up soft-shod behind them — a tall old man in a battered felt hat and shabby cloak. He must have been three score and ten at least, though still robust and upright. His face, framed by a tangled thicket of white hair, was windburnt and deeply lined.

"If you could have seen the Abbey as it once was — the sanctuary all a-glitter with gold and brass, the hangings of brocade and embroidered silk. The light through the windows casting all the colours of the rainbow over the high altars, the pillars of the nave lifting their arches up to heaven. All the lords and knights and ladies, the solemn procession of monks, the organ that played so sweetly you would swear you could hear flutes and cornets in it, and a river of plainsong winding its way to heaven."

His voice rose and fell in a sombre and familiar rhythm. *It is a litany he is chanting,* Sidonie thought. *A requiem for something precious that is lost forever.*

"All gone now, despoiled," the old man went on, as though reading her thought. "The lead stripped from the roofs, the carvings burned to melt it down. They took the gold from the altar, smashed the stained glass, carted away the very stones of the walls for road building. And then they set up a dye-house in the ruins, and moved in a company of Flemish weavers."

"And you watched all this happen?" Kit sounded a little dubious.

"Aye, lad, this was my home they pillaged and destroyed, for I was an orphan and the fathers took me in as a lad of ten. I had a fine clear voice for the singing, then, and at matins and vespers I sang God's praises with the other boys. Like a choir of angels, we were. And this place was in my blood and bone — I stayed, and gave myself into the service of the Lord. and took joy in the humblest task in the service of the Abbey, which was the service of God."

"You were a Brother," said Sidonie.

"Aye, that I was. Until King Henry dispossessed us, and sent Thomas Cromwell and his minions to drive us out, and hanged our good Abbot Whiting from the top of the Tor, and fastened his head to the Abbey gate."

"What then became of the monks?"

"Pensioned off for five pounds a year from the royal coffers. Some I dare say found livings as parish clergy. I made my own choice, for I would not take their money, nor would I renounce my faith to serve the New Religion. Nor did I wish to leave the only home I ever knew."

"You stayed here? All these years?" asked Sidonie.

"Aye, I have a cottage nearby, with a kitchen garden. I do a little clerking for the village. Better here, than in a ditch or a hedgerow, with the wild rogues and the vagabonds and other masterless men."

He stood gazing up at the gaunt ruin of the Abbey. A small wind had sprung up, with a hint of autumn in it. It toyed with his beard and blew his long white hair into his eyes. Absently he pushed it back. "I remember," he said softly, "how I polished the golden candlesticks and chalices, and the brass on the tombs, and every stroke of the chamois was an offering to the Lord God in heaven. It fair broke my heart to see our treasures carried off, and the walls crumble, and the winter wind blow between the arches."

"And yet . . . " said Sidonie, looking around the derelict Abbey garden. Steeped in the hazy yellow light of evening, there was a pleasant kind of melancholy about it, and a hint of magic. She could almost imagine voices in the pillaged choir loft singing evensong; and the scent of sun-dried grass was as sweet as incense. "It seems a peaceful place," she said.

"Aye, that it is," the old man said. "No one comes here now. I'm left to myself, with only the birds in the trees and the hares in the grass for company. We keep our secrets. Now I am an old man, and will take those secrets to the grave. But I dream sometimes of the Abbey rebuilt and its treasures restored. When that day comes, when the true faith returns to England, then I know that peace and plenty will for a long time endure."

He fell silent at last, as though lost in contemplation. Sidonie bade him a courteous goodnight, and received no answer. At last glance, in the fading light, he was gazing up at the broken tower atop the Tor, rapt and far-seeing as some ancient prophet.

As soon as they were out of earshot Kit remarked, "He may rhapsodize as he likes, but his true faith brought little enough peace to England."

There was an edge of bitterness in his voice that made Sidonie turn to look at him. He said, "You have a gentle heart, Sidonie, and I can see his fine words have seduced you. But honest men and women aplenty died in Queen Mary's martyr fires, my own kinfolk among them."

Sidonie was taken aback. "You never told me that."

"No. My father never speaks of it. But our family has been Protestant since King Henry's time, and suffered greatly for it under Mary." He shrugged and smiled at her, as though in apology for his tone. "So you see, I too have secrets."

Sidonie felt they had stumbled onto dangerous ground, and made haste to change the subject. "As does the old monk, it seems. What do you suppose he meant?"

"Where your red powder is to be found, perhaps?"

Sidonie could not tell if Kit was speaking seriously, or not. "The thought occurred to me," she said. "He has lived all his life in this place. Who better to have discovered its secrets?"

"And if true, he means to take the knowledge to the grave with him. Nay, Sidonie, I know you are loathe to look into that glass ball of yours, but that is what you came to do."

Sidonie sighed. "Tomorrow," she said. "The light is almost gone, and we have not found a place to sleep."

"We could take shelter in the Abbey," Kit suggested.

Sidonie felt a small shiver of unease run down her spine. She shook her head. "There are too many ghosts," she told him, "not least the shade of the unfortunate abbot."

In the end they found an outbuilding with its stone roof still intact. While there was still light enough to see they gathered grass and bracken for their beds, and filled their waterskins from a stream; then they shared a little bread and cheese from Kit's pack, wrapped themselves in their cloaks and fell instantly asleep.

ॐ ॐ ॐ

In the clear morning sunshine the business of scrying frightened Sidonie less. She put her hand into her apron pocket and drew out the crystal, wrapped in its layers of felted cloth. Then, with Kit watching curiously, she spread the felt over a flat stone and set the crystal on it. Crouching to gaze into its centre, she let a question, and an image, take form in her mind. *Where is the hiding place of the Red Lion?*

She was quiet for a while, puzzling over the answering image that had appeared in the crystal's heart.

"It's of no avail," she said finally, looking up. "The crystal speaks in symbols — cryptograms. Two circles linked, so as to make a third shape like an almond, or an eye — and the whole enclosed in a greater circle."

Kit came to stand behind her, peering over her shoulder at the crystal. He could see nothing, only spangles of reflected light. "Perhaps that is clue enough," Kit said. "This was an ancient place of worship — surely there will be holy symbols carved into its stones."

They spent all that morning searching the Abbey, within and without, and examining one by one the tumbled stones that had fallen away from its walls and buttresses. They found a broken cross, some fragments of coloured glass, a stone plaque carved with the words "Jesus, Maria" in ancient letters; but nothing that resembled the image in the scrying glass.

"This is a fool's journey I have brought you on," said Sidonie at last. Tired, hungry and thoroughly disheartened, she wiped her damp face with her apron and shook grey dust from the folds of her skirt. "Whatever was of value here, has long since been stolen."

For answer Kit dug into his pack and handed her the end of a loaf and a chunk of cheese. "Eat," he said. "It is not yet noon, and we have scarce begun to search."

The overgrown gardens yielded no clue, nor did the derelict outbuildings. Then, behind the Abbey, they came upon a yew-shaded pathway that led up to the Tor.

At the foot of the Tor was a deep stone-lined well shaft, filled with water nearly to its brim.

"Stop a moment," Sidonie said. "Let me get a drink." She knelt by the well, scooped up water with her hands. Then paused in surprise. "Kit, what is wrong with the water? It looks tinged with blood."

Kit crouched beside her, dipped a finger into the water, tasted it. He laughed. "Not blood, Sidonie — only minerals, which as my father could tell you, will do you no harm. There must be iron in the soil where the well-spring rises. Look, you can see the rust colour where the water has seeped into the ground." Sidonie glanced down. Sure enough, all around the well, the earth was stained rusty-red. She turned back to the well, still needing to quench her thirst. And as she turned, something — the flicker of an image in the corner of her eye — made her catch her breath, and she leaped to her feet, gripping Kit's arm. "Look there. Do you see?" How could she have failed to notice it before? Just beyond the well an ancient wind-bent yew leaned over the path. A symbol had been carved into its trunk, who knew how many centuries before, the knife-cuts raised with time like a healed scar. *Two circles linked, so as to make a third shape like an almond, or an eye.*

Sidonie bent down, scraped up a handful of soil, held it out to Kit. Her voice trembled with excitement. "Kit, this must be it. The red powder — the alchemical elixir — that Dee and Kelley found."

"It's naught but a handful of dirt," Kit said.

"But surely, the most sacred dirt in England. They do say this is where the Holy Grail is buried."

"Some say," said Kit.

Sidonie could hear the skepticism in his voice.

"My father said the red powder, the Red Lion, was made of fire and water; it was a stone, yet not a stone. A thing worthless, yet valuable beyond price. A thing unknown, yet known to everyone. Do you not see, Kit? The spring water that gushes through the well stains everything around it the colour of fire. The sand in this soil was once stone, and is no longer. Soil is known to everyone, and we think it worthless. But if one ounce of it can turn an ounce of mercury into gold . . . "

"Certes, you have missed your calling," Kit said solemnly. "You argue like a lawyer, Sidonie."

CHAPTER ELEVEN

From the hagg and hungrie goblin
That into raggs would rend ye
And the spirit that stands by the naked man
In the Book of Moones defend yee!

—Tom o' Bedlam's Song

On their homeward journey Kit and Sidonie travelled eastward as the crow flies across open fields, following footpaths and sheeptracks. Now and again they begged a ride on the back of a farmer's wagon. Just outside Salisbury, where their rough track crossed the high road, they stopped to rest, and were overtaken by a motley throng of peddlers and fortune tellers, minstrels and jugglers bound for the Salisbury market. A bear-ward led his mangy, listless animal on a chain; a family of gypsies pulled a cart piled high with their worldly goods.

Then came a straggling procession of beggars and vagrants, wandering friars, and discharged soldiers still in the faded remnants of their uniforms. Sidonie had taken her Euclid from her pocket, meaning to read awhile, but now she set it aside and watched the parade with lively interest. She had often enough seen sturdy beggars in Charing Cross, but none half so queer as these.

One man strode along bare-armed and bare-legged in a long patched cloak and high- heeled shoes, carrying a wooden dish and an iron-tipped staff. Sidonie could not help but stare at this apparition, for his limbs were covered with hideous, oozing sores. Behind him trailed a lean, hard-faced woman weighed down by a heavy pack. She had an assortment of needles and thread stuck in her cap, and as she walked she purled away at a long grubby length of knitting.

Soon after came a wayfarer with a wild-eyed frenzied look. His scrawny frame was barely covered with faded, filthy rags, and his long hair and beard had matted into clumps. Dozens of pins and nails sprouted from his sunburned arms. Approaching, he stepped off the road and stumbled towards Sidonie, clutching at her with claw-like hands. Sidonie shrank back against Kit. The beggar stared at her with mad, blind eyes. "Have you anything to give poor Tom?" he whined. "Alas, poor Tom, he is starved."

For an uncertain moment Sidonie's hand moved towards their almost empty food pouch. "Nay, you must not feed him," Kit whispered. "It's Tom o' Bedlam, he only plays at madness." Hastily Sidonie clasped her hands in her lap and shook her head. She recalled what the old monk had said, when he saw them off with a jug of ale, some apples and hard cheese, and earnest words of advice. "The roads are infested with vagabonds and wild rogues. They will do no honest work, but practise their tricks on travellers to frighten them into emptying their purses."

They gathered up the last of their provisions, and set out along the high road towards Salisbury. A mile or so farther on they met another pair of vagrants, a man and a woman, who were travelling away from the city. Save for a tattered cloak and sheepskin doublet, the man was naked above the waist. His face was daubed with mud and blood, his head wrapped round with dirty cloths, his beard tied up in rags.

Suddenly, as Sidonie came near, he flung himself headlong across her path. She watched in alarm as his meagre body writhed and jerked in the dust, his arms flailing and his mouth frothing like a rabid dog's.

"Pray help him, mistress," cried his doxy. "He has the Falling Sickness."

Sidonie, who had seen a neighbour seized by one of these fits, was already on her knees beside the man, meaning to put a stick under his tongue so he would not bite it off. She turned her head to call out to Kit, who had fallen behind to examine a wayside plant.

All at once the man reached up and clutched Sidonie by the shoulders. Startled, she tried to pull away, but his grip tightened, his fingers digging cruelly into her flesh as he forced her down. Sidonie squirmed and twisted and tried to scream. Her face was pressed into the man's chest, her nose filled with the stench of dirty sheepskin and sweat. She could hear Kit shouting as he raced toward her, and then there was a dull thud and a choked-off cry.

Her captor rolled over then, carrying Sidonie with him. Now she was flat on her back, held fast to the ground by bony knees and pinching hands, and the beggar's woman was waving a knife near her throat. Sidonie cringed, tucked her chin into her chest, tried to curl away from the blade.

Then she felt a hand fumbling at her waist. The beggar-woman, grinning, held up the pouch full of red powder and shook it in Sidonie's face, as though to taunt her. In the other hand, along with the knife, she clutched the purse that held the last of their coins. And then she darted away into the shadow of an oakwood, with her partner at her heels.

Sidonie got shakily to her feet, and looked around for Kit. He was lying by the roadside a few yards away, his head resting in a pool of blood. Choking back tears, she stumbled over to him. Kneeling, she cradled his shoulders and felt for the wound. Blood welled from a long split in his scalp. *He is killed for certain,* she thought, with sick dismay. But after a moment he opened his eyes and struggled to sit up. She let out a long, grateful breath. "Hush, keep still," she said softly, using her kerchief to wipe away the blood.

"I'll wager you could use some help."

Sidonie glanced up, saw a stranger approaching on an elegant grey mare. She had a quick impression of piercing blue eyes, a full-lipped, smiling mouth, a modishly trimmed beard.

The man dismounted, leading his horse. He moved with a courtier's confident grace.

"Indeed we could, sir. I stopped to help a man who seemed in dire distress, and this is how we were rewarded."

"What manner of distress?" Though the question was seriously enough posed, there was a glint of humour as well as concern in the young man's eyes.

"His woman said he had the Falling Sickness, and indeed, he had every symptom, with a wild look in his eye, and frothing at the mouth."

"'Struth, mistress, you're not the first traveller to be taken in by that trick. That was a Counterfeit Crank, and it was no sickness he had, only a mouthful of soapsuds. It's your purse he wanted, not your help."

"And that he got," said Sidonie glumly. "All the money I had left, and other valuables besides."

"What valuables were those?"

But Sidonie had already revealed more than she had intended. "I fear, sir, I am not at liberty to say." Her reply, meant to be courteous, sounded in her own ears pompous and self-important.

The man raised a quizzical eyebrow; and crouched down to examine Kit's head.

"He's taken a bad thump from a stick, but with luck he should live. Come, lend me a hand. I'll take him with me on my mount." Between them they got Kit to his feet. Still only half-conscious, he was a dead, uncooperative weight. The young man hoisted Kit astride the mare, then sprang lithely into the saddle behind him. Kit slumped against the man's shoulder, looking pale and dazed.

Their rescuer gathered up the reins. "My apologies, mistress, that I must make you walk. But it is no great distance to Wilton House."

"Is that where you are taking him? He needs a physician."

"And he shall have one, mistress. The finest in England. But I forget my manners entirely. I am Adrian Gilbert. And what may I call you, mistress?"

"I am called Sidonie. Sidonie Quince. And this is my brother Kit." She added hastily, "Kit Aubrey. My foster-brother, who was raised in my father's house."

"Quince. I know that name. Simon Quince the astrologer, is it not, who has been called to court while Dr. Dee remains abroad? He looked down at her. "A relative, perchance?"

"My father," Sidonie told him.

"Is he indeed, mistress? Then you must be the young woman who is to become the Queen's prognosticator."

"Then you know a great deal more than I," said Sidonie, taken aback.

"But you were at Hampton Court, and scried for Her Majesty, did you not?"

"Yes but, how did you . . . ?"

Gilbert grinned down at her. "Did you imagine because we are simple country folk, we are not privy to court gossip?"

Simple country folk indeed, thought Sidonie, observing his doublet of embroidered velvet, his fashionably padded breeches, the scarlet silk lining of his cloak. All the same he had a hale, robust look, as though he spent much of his time outdoors.

Ambling along at Sidonie's pace, he turned onto a bridle-path winding its way across the greensward. Presently the path widened and joined a tree-lined carriageway. Ahead lay a stone manor house surrounded by a high wall, with trees and gardens stretching down to the river beyond.

"Welcome to Wilton House, Sidonie Quince," said Gilbert, as she followed him though the tall arched gateway into the inner courtyard. Dismounting, he tossed the reins to a groom.

With the porter's assistance Gilbert helped Kit to the ground. "Can you walk, sir?" Kit nodded uncertainly.

By now two liveried servants had appeared. "Take him to one of the guest chambers," Gilbert told them. "And send for Lady Mary's physician to attend him." He beckoned to Sidonie, who was hanging back uncertainly. "Mistress Quince, if you please, do you come this way."

He led her along a cobbled passageway and up a spiral staircase to a pleasant, sunlit sitting room. There was a fireplace, elaborately carved with birds and fruits and classical scenes. The walls were lined with tapestries, the floor carpeted, the high plastered ceiling decorated with an exuberant pattern of vines and flowers.

"If you will excuse me," said Gilbert, "I will tell Lady Mary you are here."

Left to her own devices, Sidonie sank down on a cushioned settle. She was bone-weary, aching from head to foot, and on the edge of tears. Through misguided pity, she had lost the treasure they had risked so much to find. Must they now retrace their steps to Glastonbury, with neither food nor money to sustain them, her father soon back from London, and Kit half-killed besides?

Tired as she was, it was too much to contemplate. Kit would be cared for, his wound dressed, by more expert hands than hers; she should rest while she could. After a moment a serving maid came in with a goblet of wine and a plate of currant tarts. Sidonie drank the wine in one thirsty draught, and devoured the tarts. The unwatered wine rushed to her head and she felt her tired limbs relax. Through drooping lids she contemplated a carved scene of the goddess Diana bathing. What must it be like, she wondered, half-asleep, to live in such a grand house as this?

ॐ ॐ ॐ

"Mistress Quince, your brother is awake, and asking after you." Sidonie came to herself with a start as a tall, slender woman entered the room. She was dressed all in black, with neither jewels nor ornaments, but there was an air of rank and authority about her.

Sidonie rose hastily to her feet and managed a curtsey. "My lady?"

"You guess rightly," the woman said with a smile." I am Mary Herbert. And you, I am told, are Sidonie Quince of Charing Cross, who has had a long journey and many adventures."

Above the woman's black velvet bodice and lace-trimmed ruff, red-gold hair shone like a new-minted coin. Sidonie could see the sharp intelligence in that oval face with its sombre, wide-set eyes and broad, pale brow, already faintly etched with lines. Mary Countess of Pembroke, Sir Philip Sidney's sister: after the Queen, the second cleverest woman in England, Sidonie's father had said. Sidonie remembered those words, because he had added, only half in jest, that if Sidonie kept on with her studies she might one day be the third. *I lief would have this lady's good opinion,* Sidonie thought. But her tongue felt thick and unmanageable. She regretted that large goblet of wine, so hastily quaffed.

"Come, I will take you to your brother," said the Countess. "And afterwards, you shall have a good supper, and mayhap we will talk."

She set off at a lively pace, Sidonie following a little unsteadily, through galleries and passageways and up a flight of stairs. At length the Countess paused at a half-open doorway and glanced in.

"Ah, I see you are expected," she said with a faint smile. "Go you in, Sidonie. I will send my maid to fetch you by and by."

Kit was lying propped up on silk pillows in an immense bed with gold-embroidered curtains and fluted posts. His head was wrapped in bandages, but a healthy colour had returned to his face, and as Sidonie tiptoed into the room, he gave her a faintly sheepish grin. He sat up, pushing back the velvet coverlet, and she saw that he was wearing a splendid white linen nightshirt lavishly embellished with lace. A black damask dressing gown lay across the foot of the bed. "See what a popinjay I have become," he said. "Methinks, Mistress Sidonie, I could become well accustomed to this life."

"Oh, Kit, don't jest, I have been beside myself. What says the physician? Will you mend?"

Kit laughed. "He says it's God's mercy my skull is so thick. It's naught but a scalp wound, quickly healed, and such a headache as I never wish to have again."

"And all for my sake, who brought you on this ill-fated journey," lamented Sidonie. She sat down gingerly on the edge of the bed. Kit reached out and seized one of her hands in his.

"Grieve not on my account, fair lady. Have a sugar-plum instead." He nodded towards the bedside chest, where candied fruits and flower petals were arranged on a silver tray.

"You would comfort me with comfits," observed Sidonie, reaching for a slice of pomegranate.

"Exactly so."

"But Kit, it is worse than you know, all our money is gone, and the red powder besides."

"The money I expected, but the powder? It would seem to a beggar no more than common dirt."

"Did you not wonder if it was chance meeting with that beggar? Why should he waste his rogue's tricks on travellers as poor and footsore as us?"

"What mean you, Sidonie? That we were singled out?"

She said, "Do you remember at the inn in Salisbury, I had a fancy we were being watched? Suppose it were no fancy?"

"That is a weighty supposition, for a man with his brains already curdled."

She leaned forward impatiently, as the notion caught hold of her. "Kit, you must be serious. You know nothing of plots and palace intrigues, they have not concerned you. But the day my father was summoned to court and made promises he could not keep, he and I were drawn willy-nilly into that world."

CHAPTER TWELVE

O wonder!
How many goodly creatures are there here!
How beauteous mankind is! O brave new world
That has such people in't.
— William Shakespeare, *The Tempest.*

A little dark-haired maid-servant, clad as sombrely as her mistress, came to fetch Sidonie from Kit's room. No more than twelve or so, with wide, guileless eyes, she announced all in a rush, "I am called Alice, and Lady Mary has directed that I take you to your bedchamber, where I have prepared a bath, and after that I am to bring your supper, because you will wish to rest after such a misadventure."

"Name of mercy, Alice," exclaimed Sidonie. "Is my misadventure common knowledge, then?"

A grin, tugging at the edges of Alice's mouth, was quickly suppressed. "The cook did speak of it to the head gardener," she admitted, "and I couldn't help but overhear."

"Indeed," said Sidonie. "Well, no doubt I will soon be the subject of merriment for three counties round."

The little servant gave her a puzzled glance.

"I meant," said Sidonie, "for being so foolish, as to be taken in by a rogue's trick."

"Oh never say you are foolish, mistress," protested Alice. "My own aunt on my mother's side, who is a woman of great sense and good judgment, once gave a shilling she could ill afford out of pity for a clapperdudgeon, who had rubbed ratsbane into his own flesh so as to cover himself all over with fearsome sores . . . and here is your chamber, mistress," she added, scarcely pausing for breath.

The bedroom was filled with a delicious confusion of smells. Lavender-scented steam rose from a large wooden tub set before the hearth. Applewood crackled on the fire and on a low chest, musk burned in a censer.

"Your bath is ready," said Alice, "and I have set your night-things out."

Sidonie undressed to her smock and handed Alice her mud-stained, dusty garments. She picked up a ball of rosemary-scented soap, dropped her smock to the floor, and sank into the bathwater with a sigh of content. She felt as pampered as a queen.

While Sidonie scrubbed away the grime of her journey, Alice busied herself arranging tooth-cloth and soap on the enamelled washstand, and silver-backed ivory combs on a chest. Then she helped Sidonie wash her hair.

Sidonie leaned back against the side of the tub and gazed curiously around the room, much of which was taken up by a four-poster bed with a fringed valance and a painted headboard, across which nymphs and shepherds frolicked in a summer wood. The silk coverlet was periwinkle blue, and the hangings, edged with silver embroidery, were the deeper blue of the evening sky. The chamber was furnished as well with an ebony and silver writing table, two chairs covered in rose damask, a low chest inlaid with pearl and another with marquetry, and a rosewood chest of drawers. This was a bedchamber fit for a princess of the realm, not plain Sidonie Quince of Charing Cross.

"Come, mistress, the water is growing cool." Alice had set out a linen towel, a pair of house-slippers, a clean smock embroidered in coloured silks, and a velvet-lined blue silk dressing gown trimmed with silver lace. "If you are finished bathing I will dry your hair and comb it for you."

Sidonie, slippered and smock-clad, sat down obediently beside the fire. *What luxury is this,* she thought, as Alice rubbed her hair with a towel and patiently combed the tangles out. She tried to imagine such attentions at the hands of sharp-tongued, slapdash Emma.

"Is the household in mourning still?" asked Sidonie by way of conversation, while Alice struggled with an obstinate knot.

"Indeed yes, mistress. Alas, poor Lady Mary, it is not twelve months since Sir Philip was slain in the Netherlands. She lost her mother, her father and her brother all in the span of a year." The tangle was at last subdued and Alice waved her comb in triumph. "Such a high-spirited lady she was, and she and her brother as close as peas in a pod, and now she is so weighed down by grief that all the light has gone out of her face."

"Then surely, Alice . . . she may not look kindly on unexpected guests."

"Oh, fie, mistress, you must not worry on that account. Wilton House is always full of friends, and relatives, and visitors, and all manner of guests. They are often as not two score at table, and it is hard to tell who is family and who is not." She gave a small cluck of satisfaction. "There, now you are properly combed, do you put on your dressing gown, and I will go see if cook has your supper ready."

ॐ ॐ ॐ

Sidonie opened her eyes after a long night filled with restless dreams, and fancied she must still be dreaming. The sunlight falling through the tall narrow window threw diamonds of jewelled light, rose-red and sapphire blue and topaz, across the floor. She sat up, rubbing sleep from her eyes.

There was a soft knock on the door, and Alice came in carrying a tray. She set it down carefully on the chest beside the bed, next to a velvet-bound copy of Froissart's *Chronicle*. There was fine white manchet bread, butter spiced with nutmeg, a pot of honey and another of gooseberry preserves, orange slices, a dish of stewed pears, and a silver jug of barley water.

"I have a message from Master Aubrey," Alice said. "He bids me tell you, he is alive and well, and when you have breakfasted, he awaits you in the physic garden."

"A welcome message indeed," said Sidonie, around a mouthful of bread and honey. "But Alice, where are my clothes?"

Alice looked momentarily disconcerted. "Alas, mistress, I fear your kirtle is in a sorry state, and your petticoats little better."

"But Alice, what shall I wear? I cannot go out in my smock."

Alice giggled. "Nay, mistress, Lady Mary has gowns to spare. Do you finish your breakfast, and I will be back in a trice."

When she returned her arms were heaped with garments. There was a kirtle of fine pale green lawn worked in silver threads, an apron in ivory silk, a boned under-bodice, and a froth of petticoats to go beneath. "Lady Mary is a little taller," she said, "and a little plumper in the bosom, but these will do well enough, methinks."

When she had finished tying Sidonie's laces and pinning her ruff, she stepped back to admire her handi-work. "Marry, Mistress Sidonie, you are the very picture of a lady. But something must needs be done about your hair."

Sidonie pushed back her tumbling mass of dark brown curls. "When my hair is fresh-washed it has a mind of its own," she said ruefully.

But Alice, with a practised hand, gathered up the wayward curls, sleeked them down with rose-scented lotion, and held them in place with a velvet cap. "There," she said with brisk satisfaction." Now see." And Sidonie, who hated mirrors, could not resist a sidelong glance. A slender, elegant figure in green looked out at her from the glass. Sidonie stared bemusedly back. She scarcely recognized herself. "Now, mistress, " prompted Alice, "you must tarry not a moment longer, it is a rare fine day, and Master Aubrey is waiting."

ॐ ॐ ॐ

Sidonie strolled in her borrowed finery across the long green lawns. There was no need to hurry; Kit would be happily occupied for hours among the Countess's botanicals. And so she wandered, pleasantly distracted, through knot gardens bright with late summer flowers, along grassy paths, through arbours and walkways shaded by honeysuckle and clematis. At the far end of a lawn two young men were playing noisy tennis. Further on, beyond a clipped yew hedge, she came upon a game of bowls, the players in their summer silks and feathered hats as gorgeous as the peacocks that strutted on the nearby grass. Presently she climbed a flight of moss-grown steps to a terrace, where a man was deadheading roses. Imagining him for one of the servants, Sidonie was about to ask for directions. Then he looked up, secateurs in hand, and she was startled to find that the gardener was Adrian Gilbert. Today he wore no silks and velvets, only plain workman's breeches and jerkin, and a broad-brimmed felt hat to keep the sun off his face.

"Mistress Quince, I bid you good morning." He made an elegant leg, whipped off his hat and swept it low.

"Good morning to you, Master Gilbert." Should she curtsey? Sidonie wondered. How little prepared she was for life in these exalted circles! She settled for a courteous nod. "Sir, you took me quite by surprise."

"Oh, you will often find me in the gardens. I do what little I can to earn my keep. But tell me, Mistress Quince, does all go well with Master Aubrey, and with yourself?"

"Happily, Kit is mending, " Sidonie replied. "Thanks to your kindness, and the skill of Lady Mary's physician. But as for me, sir . . . I fear I am in a sore predicament."

"How so?" He gazed at her with genuine concern.

"I needs must return to Glastonbury, to replace what was stolen from me . . . " She saw Gilbert's raised brows, knew he was waiting for an explanation, offered none. "As well I must be back in Charing Cross before my father returns from London."

"A quandary indeed, to be in two places at once," said Gilbert. "But easily enough solved, I think. Do you ride, Mistress Sidonie?"

"Kit does. I fancy I can stay on a horse, if he be well-mannered."

Gilbert laughed. "Honestly spoke," he said. "So then. We will find you the most amiable beast in Lady Mary's stables, and as soon as the physician declares Master Aubrey fit to ride, you shall be away to Glastonbury. And as for your return to London, Lady Mary intends to travel there by coach in a few days' time. There will be room and to spare for you and Master Aubrey."

"But you are all so kind to us," declared Sidonie with relief and gratitude. "Lady Mary has treated two bedraggled strangers as though we were her own kinfolk."

"Bedraggled you may have been," said Gilbert. "But hardly strangers. Your reputation precedes you, Mistress Quince."

Sidonie puzzled over those words. What reputation could she have, among these clever, courtly folk? The service she had done the Queen was paltry enough, considering that she had scried no more than the Queen already guessed.

And then, as she was bidding Gilbert good day, she had a disconcerting thought. Out of ambition and foolish pride her father had sworn to make gold for the royal coffers. What other rash promises might he have made, that Sidonie would be required to keep?

At length she came to the physic garden, a sun-drenched enclosure heady with the scents of sage and thyme, lavender and rosemary. Late-blooming borage, marigolds, rose campion made a bright display against the soft plum colour of the old brick walls. Kit was on his knees, examining a plant with that particular intensity he reserved for growing things. He glanced up as Sidonie approached. "Sidonie Quince, can that be you? I swear, you look like Lady Greensleeves."

She laughed. "It seems I am to be duchess for a day. Tomorrow I expect I will be plain Sidonie again. But Kit, are you quite recovered?"

"My head thrums like a lute string if I move too quickly, but the physician tells me that will pass."

Save for the bandage round his head, he seemed his usual stalwart self. "Look you, Sidonie, this is such a garden as I have only dreamed of." Wincing a little as he got to his feet, he seized her by the hand and guided her among the bricked-edged plots, pointing out the rarest specimens.

"See, here are apples of love from Spain, and madde apples nearly ripened. There is mandrake in that corner, over here white hellebore from the Alps, tiger lilies all the way from Constantinople . . . scores of plants, Sidonie, that I have only read about in herbals."

She laughed, enjoying his excitement. "Study them well while you may," she said, "for on the morrow, if you are well enough to ride, we return to Glastonbury. Master Gilbert has offered to lend us horses."

"You have never ridden a horse," Kit pointed out.

"I will learn. I do not mean to go home empty handed."

She was silent for a moment, watching a cloud of butterflies dancing in a stand of goldenrod. In this peaceful autumn garden with its tidy geometric beds, all was order and reason. Here, humankind and nature seemed in perfect accord. Yet in some corner of her mind there stirred a faint unease.

Finally she said, "Kit, do you not find it curious, how we have been made so welcome here?"

"Curious? What mean you, Sidonie? One could not have asked for more gracious hosts."

"I meant only that we are strangers, with no special place in society, ragged and travel-stained to boot. Surely in most great houses we would have been sent like beggars to the kitchen door, not treated as honoured guests."

"Sidonie, you think too little of yourself. You are a learned woman, as the Countess is, and besides, this is no ordinary house. It is like a little Oxford — there are scholars and poets visiting from every corner of England. Sidonie, now that you have been to court, you see plots and machinations behind every bush."

"When *you* have been to court," retorted Sidonie, "you will see that there *are* plots and machinations behind every bush. Kit, these are no idle fancies of mine, this is a world ruled by plots and politics, and it can be death to misplace your trust."

CHAPTER THIRTEEN

Histories make men wise; poets witty; the mathematics subtile; natural philosophy deep; moral, grave; logic and rhetoric, able to contend.

— Francis Bacon, *On Studies*

In the forenoon Alice brought another summons — for summons it was, Alice's tone made clear, and not an invitation. If Mistress Quince pleased, would she repair to the library? "Lady Mary sends her apologies," Alice added, with a hint of self-importance, "for she has been at prayer all the morning, but now she is free, and wishes to speak with you."

So many audiences, and I so ill-prepared, thought Sidonie as she followed Alice nervously down the stairs and along the maze of ground-floor corridors. In the library, heavy linen curtains were drawn against the afternoon sun. Bookshelves lined the walls, and in the centre of the room stood an oak table supplied with writing materials and a pair of silver candlesticks. After a moment a servant entered, carrying a flagon of wine, two glasses and a dish of comfits on a pewter tray. Alice took the tray and set it on the table, drew up two high-backed cushioned chairs, and went out, leaving Sidonie to her own devices.

Delighting in the familiar perfume of calfskin and morocco leather, Sidonie prowled from shelf to shelf, reading the gold-tooled spines. She glanced with scant attention at the works of poetry and romance, resplendent in their red velvet bindings and jewel-ornamented silver clasps; moved on past the herbals and histories, the tomes on hunting, heraldry and hawking; and paused before a tall case filled with works of science and mathematics, many of them bound in heavy old-fashioned boards, and all of them seemingly well-read. Here were volumes in Greek and Latin, as well as translations into modern tongues: works of cosmography, mathematics, astronomy, natural history. Boethius, Galen and Copernicus shared the crowded shelves with Theon of Alexandra, Regiomontanus, the *De re medica* of Celsus, Aristotle's *Meteorologica*, the *Origines* of Isadore of Seville. There were many works as well on alchemy — some familiar to Sidonie, others she recognized as rare volumes, almost impossible to obtain. *What my father would give to own such treasures,* she thought.

A soft voice spoke from the doorway. "Mistress Sidonie, I see you take an interest in mathematics."

Sidonie, who was crouching to explore a bottom shelf, got hastily to her feet and, still holding a volume of Alhazen of Basra in Latin translation, managed a curtsey. "Yes, my lady."

The Countess, pale and regal in black silk, waved her to a chair. "You may borrow that book if you wish. I fancied myself a mathematician, once — a true daughter of Hypatia. But I confess I was no more than an amateur — it seems my talents lay elsewhere."

Sidonie accepted a glass of wine and a comfit. "My lady, you know what Roger Bacon says. 'Nobody can attain to proficiency in the science of mathematics unless he devotes to its study thirty or forty years . . . '"

" . . . and that is the reason there are so few mathematicians," Lady Mary finished for her. "And do you intend to devote as much time as that to the study, Mistress Quince?"

"If God grants me so many years," replied Sidonie.

Lady Mary seemed to hear something more in that polite response than was intended. Her eyes gleamed with sudden tears and her voice trembled as she said, "My dear, I only pray He will." As quickly regaining her composure, she added, "We must be thankful for what time we are given, I suppose — though sometimes it is hard to accept the fates of those we love with a good grace." Then, as though picking up the thread of some earlier conversation, she remarked, "Master Gilbert speaks uncommonly well of you."

"Indeed?" said Sidonie, disconcerted. "I am flattered, my lady."

"I value his opinion. We have much in common, Master Gilbert and I. He too lost a brother who died in the service of the Queen."

Sidonie realized, then, why Adrian's name had seemed familiar. "Of course, how foolish of me — his brother was Sir Humphrey Gilbert, who was shipwrecked on the Squirrel. They say he died with the words, 'We are as near to heaven by sea as by land.'"

"A hero's death," said Lady Mary, with a certain lack of conviction. "As Adrian will tell you, being kin to a dead hero is a matter of pride on great occasions, when you hear his praise on everyone's lips — but small enough comfort when you see his empty place at table."

Sidonie felt a sudden weight in her chest. Though the years had dulled the shock of her mother's death, Lady Mary's words brought it back like a knife-thrust. *My mother was a hero too,* she thought, *and there will always be an empty place at my father's table.*

"The only comfort for me now is to carry on my brother's fight by whatever means I can," said Lady Mary. "It is gold that will defeat Spain — gold to build more ships and arm them, gold to provision Her Majesty's Navy. If I were a man, I would go to sea, and plunder the Spanish galleons for their treasure. Or like Humphrey Gilbert I would seek a passage through the frozen seas to the gold of Cathay. But we are women, Sidonie. We cannot go to sea, nor take up the sword for England. We must find other ways to serve."

Sidonie set down her glass. It seemed to her they were treading on familiar ground. "My lady, forgive me if I mistake your meaning — is it possible you speak of alchemy?"

"And why should you think that, Sidonie Quince?"

Sidonie met Lady Mary's level grey gaze, and to her relief saw no offence, only curiosity.

"It is just that my father has often praised your knowledge of chemistry. And I remember his saying that Dr. Dee has been a visitor to Wilton, and you to Mountlake."

"Are all my secrets common knowledge, then?" The Countess's voice was good-humoured. "Yes, I often visited Dr. Dee at Mountlake. I confess as well to some knowledge of chemistry, and Master Gilbert — you realize, Sidonie, I am trusting you with secrets — is a student of the occult arts. Like others, we dreamed of infinite riches, unlimited power, eternal life. We had a well-equipped laboratory, and the use of Dr. Dee's library, the best in England, far surpassing what you see on these shelves. And still we failed — as so many have failed before us. The philosopher's stone eluded our grasp. So you see, once I might have spoken of alchemy, but no longer."

At that moment it was on the edge of Sidonie's tongue to share her own secret, to tell the Countess of the red powder that could turn all the seas to molten gold. But something — discretion, uncertainty — made her hold back. Suppose she were wrong after all, and the red elixir was no more than it seemed — a handful of common dirt. If she appeared a fool to the rest of the world, it scarcely mattered. But she could not abide the thought of losing Mary Herbert's good opinion.

"The only alchemy I practise now," said Lady Mary, "is the alchemy of words. But you, Sidonie — can you be persuaded to use *your* talent to serve the Queen?"

Sidonie started, almost spilling her wine.

"My lady, I am no alchemist."

Lady Mary held up a long, pale hand. "No, hear me out, Sidonie. I speak not of alchemy, but of your gift for seeing what is hidden."

"You speak of hidden gold, my lady?"

"Just so. When King Henry turned the monks out of Glastonbury and seized the treasures of the Abbey, there was much that was never accounted for."

Sidonie gazed at the Countess in sudden comprehension, and no little dismay. "We keep our secrets," the old monk had said. "I will take those secrets to the grave."

Lady Mary continued, "In earlier times Adrian was often at Mountlake, and he knows what secrets can be revealed by a clever scryer. But who can we trust? Occultists on the whole are a dubious lot — one need only think of the Venetian charlatan Giovanni Agnello, who found a bit of fool's gold in a lump of rock, and persuaded all London that King Solomon's mine had been discovered in Cathay."

Sidonie laughed. Everyone knew that story. Her mother had oftentimes reminded Simon Quince of it, when he became too immoderate in his aspirations. "And Martin Frobisher set out with fifteen ships to bring back ore from the New World, and all of it ended up as paving stones."

"But you, Sidonie Quince — I think you honest, and a loyal subject of the Queen."

Lady Mary rose to her feet, a frail, slender, imperious presence. Her eyes were large and pleading in her pretty, grief-worn face. "There is a prophecy, that when the Glastonbury treasure is found, peace will be assured for England. Methinks it was not mere happenchance that brought you here, Sidonie Quince, Methinks it were the hand of God."

And then, as Sidonie struggled to find a response, the Countess said, "But finish your wine, my dear, and we will speak more of this later. The weather is so fine that I think we will dine in the summerhouse this eve. Who knows how many more chances there will be, before the autumn rains come? Just a simple meal with friends, and we will make our own entertainment after."

ॐ ॐ ॐ

The summer house stood amid banks of lilies, lavender and rosemary in a walled garden that still held the lingering warmth of afternoon. Within were cushioned benches, drawn up to a long oak table laid with a damask cloth. Somewhere nearby a lutenist played a sprightly air.

Some twenty guests had gathered. Most were resplendent in jewel-coloured silks, tissue of gold and silver lace, though a few wore sober gowns befitting their greater age and dignity. Sidonie, in a lace ruff and a borrowed silk gown the colour of carnations, found a place and sat down, with Kit on her left, and on her right a quiet young man in brown velvet.

So enthralled was Sidonie with the glint of torchlight on silver plate and Venetian glass, the mingled scents of herbs and flowers, the gorgeous apparel of the dinner guests, that she almost forgot to eat. She had scarcely tasted her petal-strewn salad of borage and endive, when a seemingly endless succession of hot dishes arrived.

"A simple meal, sitting down with friends," Lady Mary had said. Sidonie thought wryly of her own sparse table, as she was offered venison in sour cream, ox tongue in saffron, boiled crab and lobster, several varieties of fish in numerous sorts of exotic sauces, and other delicacies she had yet to identify.

Kit had told Sidonie that the cleverest minds in England — chemists, astrologers, physicians, botanists, historians — sat down together at Lady Mary's table. However, it seemed that tonight it was art, not science, holding sway. The thin, pale gentleman visiting from Dublin had been introduced as Master Edmund Spenser, author of the famous *Shepherd's Calendar*. Sir John Davies, the musician, was there, and Michael Drayton, who was a poet — soon to be a published one, he declared. He had brought along his friend Will — the young man on Sidonie's right — who was also a poet, and a Warwickshire man like himself. *Speak to me of angles and hypotenuses,* thought Sidonie, *and I will acquit myself well enough.* Alas, tonight the talk was all of versification.

The conversation was held captive for a while by a young man in an elaborately slashed and embroidered doublet, and a beard dyed straw-yellow to match his costume. He was, he explained, composing an epic romance in verse, telling of marvels he had seen when travelling in the Isles of Spice. There, he swore, he had witnessed such sights as few men live to tell about: houses built of ambergris and pearl, parrots who played chess and discoursed in philosophy, dancing geese and children born from eggs. In those enchanted isles lived dogs with the hands and feet of men, and three-headed flying serpents, and men with no heads at all who wore their eyes in the middle of their breasts.

"Dragons there are in Ethiopia, ten fathoms long," quoted Sidonie to Kit, behind her hand. "If one is unable to invent new tales, one really ought to steal from obscure authors." Kit laughed. He too recognized Pliny's *Natural History:* he and Sidonie had pored over its pages, when they first learned to read.

"Still, a good tale is always worth the retelling," observed Michael Drayton's Warwickshire friend, who clearly had overheard her remark. She turned to him in some embarrassment. He gave her an encouraging smile. "There are, after all, a finite number of stories to be told."

"And you, sir, are you a storyteller?"

"Like Master Drayton, I dabble in sonneteering," he replied with a gallant pretence at modesty.

Sidonie had no great interest in romantic verse, and was feeling all at sea. Kit was no help: he was now deep in herbal lore with a botanist across the table. Casting about for a reply, she remembered that Sir Philip Sidney was a famous poet as well as a great hero. "And Lady Mary's brother — he too wrote sonnets," she ventured.

"Indeed," said her companion with enthusiasm, "he was the finest poet that ever was. None of us here will ever hold a candle to him. And you, Mistress Quince, do you also write poetry?" His high scholar's forehead and piercing hazel eyes gave him an air of earnest inquiry. Sidonie realized that for Will of Warwickshire, this was no idle question, but a matter of serious importance.

She blushed and shook her head. In such company, she felt awkward and tongue-tied as a milkmaid sitting down to dine with princes.

"I fear I am no scholar, sir. I have read a little mathematics, that is all."

"Then, Mistress, do not say you are no scholar. To study mathematics takes a keener mind than to write a pretty sentiment and make it scan. Pray, what attracts you to so exacting a discipline?"

Now Sidonie felt on safer ground. She thought a moment. "Its clarity," she said. She hesitated. "Its lack of ambiguity. An equation has not many possible solutions, but only one. And no matter how complex the question, if one persists long enough, an answer may be found."

"I think," said her companion, "that you speak not just of mathematics, but of truth. That is what we poets seek all our lives to discover, and some of us lose our souls in the attempt. And you, Mistress Sidonie, who swear you are no scholar and no poet, have already found the secret." He raised his goblet of delicate Venetian glass, and declared with great solemnity, "Sidonie Quince, I drink to you, and to mathematics, to beauty, and to truth!" He slurred her name a little, and she realized that he was slightly drunk.

Just then the young man who sat across the table, a student of theology at Oxford, began to praise Lady Mary's translations of the Psalms into English verse; and Sidonie, relieved, lapsed into attentive silence.

Later, as they were eating spiced figs and almond cakes, and sipping sweet Spanish alicante, there was music: some of the guests had put together a broken consort of lute, cittern, bandora, viol and flute, and others of the company sang Italian madrigals, their woven voices rising into the fragrant dark. Presently the rest of the dinner guests were invited to perform, and Adrian Gilbert sang "Robin is to the Greenwood gone" in a clear, accomplished tenor, accompanying himself on the lute.

Sidonie wondered if Lady Mary, so lately bereaved, might take offence at all this gaiety; but sitting quietly at the head of the banquet table, the Countess paid close heed to the conversation flowing about her, joining in from time to time, and listening to the music with grave appreciation.

Afterwards some of the company sat over cards and claret, while others drifted away in couples to wander the moonlit paths. And as conversation faded and the moon rode high over the walls of Wilton House, the Countess herself took up the lute and began to play: a slow and wistful melody.

O my heart and O my heart!
My heart it is so sore,
Since I must needs from my love depart
and know no cause wherefore.

Sidonie felt her throat tighten, tears sting her eyes; she could only guess from what depths of sorrow rose that bittersweet song.

CHAPTER FOURTEEN

'Tis now the very witching time of night.

—William Shakespeare, *Hamlet*

Still wakeful after midnight, Sidonie got out of bed and
threw wide the casement, leaning out into the cool
September dark. She felt hot and irritable, and her back
ached. *I'm stiff from the journey,* she persuaded herself;
tomorrow I will stay long abed, and rest.

But — and the thought brought her wide awake, every
muscle tensed — tomorrow she must scry for the Countess.
Surely that was the reason her thoughts were all a-jumble
and her limbs would not lie still.

Clearly, if there was hidden gold at Glastonbury, it was
Sidonie's duty as an Englishwoman to discover it. And
yet . . . there rose before her the face of the old monk, faith-
fully guarding the last of the treasures he held so dear. To
serve England and the Queen, she must betray him.

ॐ ॐ ॐ

Alice had spread a red silk cloth on the library table, and
pulled up a cushioned chair for Sidonie. Drawn curtains
shut out the morning sun. Sidonie unwrapped the crystal,
set it in the centre of the cloth. Then she asked Alice, who
was hovering attentively, to light a single candle.

"Thank you, Alice," Sidonie said, when all was ready. She took her handkerchief from her pocket and wiped her forehead, which, in spite of the shadowy coolness of the room, was sheened with sweat. "Do you leave me now, and close the door."

Alice gave her a conspiratorial look and tiptoed out. Sidonie heard the creak of the heavy oak door as it swung shut.

She sat for a long time in the half-lit room, comforted a little by the familiar smells of beeswax and old leather. Her head hurt, and her breakfast sat in the pit of her stomach like a leaden weight. Too much rich food at supper, she thought.

She rested her elbows on the table, cupped her chin in her hands, tried hard to concentrate. This morning her head seemed full of darting, disconnected thoughts. For a long time she could see nothing in the crystal but a flicker of candle flame. Once or twice she thought she glimpsed the gaunt walls of Glastonbury Abbey, or the thrusting shape of the Tor, but before she could make sense of the images they dissolved like mist in sunlight.

Mostly she was aware of the pain behind her eyes and in the base of her skull. What had begun as a dull, annoying ache was sharpening into agony. She felt as though claws were digging into her brain.

She straightened, pressing her hands into the small of her back, which had begun to hurt intolerably. More sweat had sprung out on her brow, soaking her hair under the front of her velvet cap, and running into her eyes.

Standing, she felt giddy and sick. *I must lie down*, she thought. *I will sleep awhile, and it will pass off.* With a great effort she made her way to the door of the library, and realized that she no longer had any idea where, in this labyrinth of halls and corridors, she should search for her bedchamber.

"Alice," she tried to call out, but she seemed to have lost her voice along with her wits.

In a daze she set out at random along a corridor. She came to a flight of stairs, but stopped, exhausted, on the third step, her heart hammering and sweat pouring down her face.

"Mistress, whatever ails you?" An anxious voice, and then an arm around her waist, steadying her as she swayed.

"Alice, thank heaven . . . I am come over all queer, Alice, I think I must lie down."

"Indeed you must, mistress. The sooner the better."

"Where is my bedchamber, Alice?" The words came out in a gasp.

"Oh mistress, it is the other side of the house, you will never walk so far. Do you hang on tight to the baluster, while I fetch Alfred. Never fear, I will be back in a trice."

Sidonie clung to the handrail while the world spun sickeningly round her. After a moment she heard running feet.

"I will fetch Dr. Moffett." Alice's voice, sounding frightened. "Do you take her to the Blue Room." A murmured response. And then Sidonie felt herself lifted in strong arms and carried along passageways, up a flight of stairs, along another passage. She had only the vaguest memory, later, of being undressed and put to bed; of figures hovering over her, someone laying a cool cloth on her forehead, someone else holding a cup of something bitter-tasting to her lips.

ॐ ॐ ॐ

Sidonie woke alone, in darkness. Her head felt as though an iron band girdled it, and a deep relentless ache gnawed at her bones. She had thrown back all her bed covers, and now lay with chattering teeth in her thin, sweat-soaked shift. There was a midwinter chill in the air. She turned her head, saw a thin grey light seeping through the window. *It is past time I was out of bed,* she thought. *Emma has overslept again and no one has lit the fire.*

She put her bare feet to the floor. A shaft of pain speared through the base of her skull, and she staggered, almost falling. She clutched hold of a bedpost and drew herself upright, then, as the dizziness receded a little, made her way by the wan light to the open door. She could see the dim outlines of furniture, but nothing seemed to be in its usual place. The windows looked all wrong. The ceiling of her dormer room, that should have been low and slanting, soared high overhead, and where was the curtained corner where lazy Emma slept?

Sidonie reached with both hands for the door frame and stepped through into the passage where the top of the staircase ought to be. But there was no staircase, and the passage itself seemed to stretch away for an impossible distance.

Now utterly disoriented, she stumbled down the hallway. Where doors stood open, she glimpsed tall, elegant rooms with canopied beds and opulent hangings.

How strange, she thought confusedly. *Our cottage seemed so small . . . how peculiar that I never came upon these rooms before . . .*

At the end of the passage, a strip of light glimmered under a closed door. Sidonie could hear a woman's voice rising and falling in a measured cadence. *It is my mother at her prayers,* she thought, her heart racing with a feverish joy. She lifted the latch, pushed open the door. "Mother . . . " she cried out. "Mother, it is me, it is Sidonie!" The words froze in her throat. It was not her mother who knelt there, but Lady Mary. She was clad in a thin white shift with a wreath of vervain upon her brow, her russet hair flowing loose upon her shoulders, and candlelight flickering on her upturned face. Before her, on a low chest, was an open book and a small enamelled case; beside the chest, a brazier from which there rose a pungent column of smoke. Sidonie recognized, from long familiarity, the mingled scents of burning hemlock, aloes wood, poppy juice and mandrake. Surrounding all was a wide circle drawn in charcoal.

The room was filled with shadow, and candle flame, and eddying smoke, and incense. Everything had the shifting, elusive quality of dreams, and yet Sidonie was sure she was not sleeping. The edge of the door, as she gripped it, felt solid under her hand. Her bones ached, her breath felt tight in her chest, her heart pounded, as they never did in dreams.

Intent upon her ritual, Lady Mary neither stirred nor looked round. It was no Christian prayer she chanted, but an invocation to older, darker gods.

. . . *Cerberus opens his triple jaw, and fire chants the praises of God with the three tongues of the lightning. The soul revisits the tombs, the magical lamps are lighted . . .* Lady Mary's voice rose, and fell, and rose again. From time to time she reached out to drop more twigs into the brazier, and white smoke billowed up.

A clammy sweat had broken out all over Sidonie's body; her head thrummed with pain. Dizzy and sick but unable to draw her eyes away, she leaned unnoticed against the door frame.

And then, in the swirling smoke, a shape began to form. In the beginning there was only a clotting of shadow against the candlelit wall, the vague suggestion of a human form. Then gradually, as Sidonie stared, it gathered substance.

There was detail now, and texture — the rich nap of the black velvet doublet, the wide silver-edged ruff, the long face with its full-lipped mouth, the dark eyes that gazed at them with gentle melancholy. And the crimson stain blossoming on the black-clad thigh.

In the hush of midnight came Mary Herbert's cry of love and anguish. The tracks of tears shone on her upturned face. She held out her arms, and soundlessly her brother moved toward her, formless spirit clothed in a semblance of flesh. He bent as though to kiss Lady Mary's brow; then painfully straightening, turned towards Sidonie. For an instant his eyes looked directly into hers. She saw his lips move, but without sound. She saw the muscles of his throat and jaw tense, as though in an attempt to speak. *But the dead cannot speak*, Sidonie thought; and wondered where she had acquired that certain knowledge.

He lifted his hands, spread them wide, dropped them to his sides in an all too human gesture of frustration. And then he took a quill from Lady Mary's writing case, dipped it in ink, opened the book that lay on the chest before her, and wrote.

Curiously, at this moment, Sidonie felt no unease, no apprehension: only sadness, and a vague astonishment at the strangeness of things. And then with Philip Sidney's sorrowful gaze still fixed upon her, her knees gave way, the room spun round, and she tumbled into darkness.

ॐ ॐ ॐ

At first, there was only darkness — a hot, smothering, inky blanket, clogging her mouth and nostrils, lying like a dead weight upon her chest.

Then the visions came.

Out of the black depths of her fever crawled a crude, misshapen mannequin forked like a mandrake root, a charred black rotting thing reduced to the barest semblance of a man. In horror and disgust she tried to flee as it staggered towards her on its half-formed limbs, but her feet were mired in wet clay, and she could not move.

All at once the darkness rolled back and the world was flooded with a luminous ice-cold light. A gibbous moon hung low on the horizon. Sidonie reached out and seized it with both hands but like quicksilver it slid from her grasp. And then she was walking through a vast arched space where rooms endlessly unfolded into other rooms. Everywhere there were mirrors, and in each one, other mirrors were reflected, infinitely receding.

She found herself in a library, where every book was written in some indecipherable foreign script; where gramaries, herbals, works of mathematics lay scattered beneath her feet like broken tiles.

Bells chimed a long way off, and she knew she was late for a wedding, though whether it was her own, or Lady Mary's, or the Queen's, she could not recall. Seized by a feverish urgency, she hurried from room to room. The corridors were lined with statues of heraldic beasts —

leopards, panthers, griffins, dragons. They snapped and snarled at her as she passed.

Now she came to a walled garden where a copper-haired woman sat by the edge of a pool. Her skin was as pale as milk and her gown was the red of cinnabar. She looked up at Sidonie with topaz-yellow eyes. "They call this chamber Paradise," she said. "Sidonie Quince, where is my gold?"

Lost in her fever-dream Sidonie rushed on, until she found herself at last inside a cavern with curving walls and roof of glass, walled round with flame. She could not breathe in that furnace-heat. It seared her skin, set her hair aflame; her flesh dripped away like tallow. And there in the midst of the flames stood a lion with a burning mane and wings as red as pomegranate seeds. She leaped astride his back, clutched his fiery mane. Together they broke through the walls of glass, soared higher and higher, until they flew into the golden mirror of the sun and were consumed.

ॐ ॐ ॐ

There was a murmur of voices. She felt cool fingers pressed to her brow.

"The fever has broken," a man's voice said. "By God's grace the worst is over, I think."

Another, younger voice. Kit's voice, surely? "But she is still unconscious?"

"No, merely asleep, now. A wholesome sleep, at last."

Sidonie opened her eyes. She stared up at the plaster foliage on the ceiling, blinking hard until its blurred outlines sharpened.

"Sidonie . . . " She turned her head on the damp pillow. Why did Kit sound so tired, so anxious? His face, as he leaned towards her, looked thinner and paler than she remembered. There were dark circles under his eyes.

She struggled to sit up, feeling weak and light-headed. The effort made sweat spring out on her forehead and she fell back, exhausted.

"Kit — what has happened to me?" The words came out in a hoarse whisper.

"You have been ill," Kit said gently, "Quite out of your head for three days, and worrying us half to death."

"But what is this place?"

"You are at Wilton House, and thanks to the good Dr. Moffett" — he nodded to the physician, who, looking grave but relieved, was standing at the foot of the bed — "it seems you will live."

Memory came flooding back. She struggled to lift herself up on her elbows. The room swam. "Wait," Kit said, and he pushed an embroidered cushion behind her back. "Lie still, Sidonie. There is nothing you must do now but rest."

"But Kit — three days! What will my father think, when he returns from London and finds me gone?"

"Fear not, Lady Mary has sent a most devious message to Charing Cross. She has written to your father that she was in need of a scryer, and sent for you in his absence, and that you fell ill, but are recovering. Much of which is true."

"Mistress Sidonie?" A small hushed sickroom voice. Sidonie turned her head, saw Alice tiptoeing into the room. "Oh, mistress, I am so happy to see you returned to your senses."

"Truly, Alice, I have been asleep for three days?"

"'Struth, Mistress Sidonie. But it was no proper slumber. All the while you threshed, and flung yourself about, and raved like Tom o' Bedlam."

"Raved, Alice?"

"Aye, mistress, you had a great deal to say, and not a jot of sense in any of it."

"Of what did I speak, Alice?"

"Oh, of everything, and nothing. Of mirrors, and moons, and ghosts, and all manner of nonsensical things."

Sidonie felt a sudden release, a weight lifting from her chest. The world, after all, was a rational place, where the dead lay quiet in their graves. Sir Philip's ghost had been nothing more than a fever-vision, that would soon fade like the other chimeras crowding her overheated brain.

She took a few sips of the barley water that Alice had brought her, let Alice wash her face and comb her draggled hair, then lay back on the pillows and drifted into dreamless sleep.

ॐ ॐ ॐ

"What a fright you gave us, Mistress Quince!"

It was Adrian Gilbert, no longer wearing workman's garb but elegantly clad in chestnut hose and a doublet of tawny velvet. He was smiling broadly, and carrying a pewter posset cup on a tray.

Sidonie, now propped up with a surfeit of cushions and wrapped in a brocade dressing-gown, accepted the cup, and took a cautious sip. 'Til now she had recoiled at the thought of food, or any drink but barley water. But this concoction, smelling pleasantly of flowers and spices, seemed at once to settle her stomach and clear her head.

"Tell me, what is this magic elixir, Master Gilbert?"

"Why, it is my own invention, Adrian Gilbert's Cordialle Water, an infallible remedy for colic, consumption, fevers, measles, pox . . . not to mention swooning and disorders of digestion."

"And may I be told what it contains?"

"Mistress Quince, you are far too curious — but this much I will reveal: roses, cinnamon, gillyflowers, peaches and sundry other ingredients, distilled and mixed with civet, musk, and ambergris . . . but the secret is in the powdered unicorn's horn."

Sidonie laughed, not sure whether he spoke in jest. "Certes, it is the unicorn's horn that is restoring me to health. Are you then a physician as well as a gardener and a chemist, Master Gilbert?"

"Nay, the diagnoses I leave to Dr. Moffett — but chemistry too is a branch of medicine."

"And besides the swooning, from which of that long list of ailments have you cured me?"

His smile faded. "At first Dr. Moffett feared smallpox, or worse yet the plague, but by God's mercy, it proved not so. He suspects you may have taken some fever from the poisoned breath of the beggar who accosted you." He drew up a chair to the bedside and sat down. "Giddiness, headache, an excess of perspiration, all are symptoms of the sweating sickness, though Dr. Moffett swears there has been no case in England since Edward's time. If in truth it was sweating sickness, you have had a miraculous escape."

"Indeed," said Sidonie, "I sweated so much it is a wonder there is anything left of me but a dry husk." She held up the empty posset cup. "And I have a fearful thirst. Perchance, is there any more of this wizard's brew?"

Gilbert laughed. "In good time, Mistress Quince. Too much at once, and we will have you dancing the *volte* in your bed-slippers. I'll be back this evening. And see, you have another visitor waiting."

Sidonie glanced round, saw Lady Mary hovering in the doorway, looking more than usually forlorn. "My lady!"

"Dr. Moffett tells me you are much improved."

"Indeed she is, Lady Mary," Gilbert said. "A miraculous recovery, for which we may all be grateful." With a sweeping bow first to Sidonie, and then to Lady Mary, he strode out in obvious high spirits.

"My lady, do sit down."

"Yes," said the Countess, vaguely. She gathered up her skirts and sank into the bedside chair. "I have prayed for you, Sidonie. We have all prayed. Thank heaven those prayers were answered." She held one of Sidonie's hands in her cool, dry grasp. "But how quickly the young heal. You look almost your old self."

"Master Gilbert has been cossetting me with his potions, my lady."

"Yes," said Mary Herbert, with a faint smile. "They work magic, those concoctions of his. Would he could mend hearts as easily."

"My lady?"

The Countess's fingers tightened on Sidonie's. "You were there. You saw."

"My lady, I know not where I was, or what I saw. Dr. Moffett says I wandered in my sleep, and that I had a fever-dream . . . "

"You know that what you saw was no dream, Sidonie — though it might have been for all the comfort it brought me. Though my arms ache to embrace him, he is nothing but shadow and smoke, that vanishes at my touch."

Poor lady, thought Sidonie. *In her grief, she can no longer tell what is a dream, and what is real.* And yet, she thought in lingering confusion, how strange that she and the Countess should have shared the self-same vision.

"You must let him go," said Sidonie, with a wisdom she hadn't known she possessed.

"God knows I have tried," said Lady Mary. "But each night I cast the spells anew, hoping for the sound of his voice, the touch of his hand — for consolation." She leaned forward. Her green eyes had a hectic, feverish look. "My child, you must promise you will not betray me. What I did was against the laws of both God and man."

Sidonie said softly, "Surely God will forgive you, knowing you acted out of love."

"God perhaps, if He is as merciful as you imagine. But if I am found out, will the courts forgive me?"

"According to the statute, my lady, it is only a felony if the spirits you invoke are evil ones."

The Countess gave her a wry smile. "So not to be hung, then, but only gaoled and pilloried? But Sidonie Quince, you seem uncommonly well acquainted with the law."

"So would you be, my lady, if you were the daughter of Simon Quince." And then, with a pang of conscience, Sidonie remembered the task she had left undone. "Forgive me, Lady Mary, I promised to scry for you, but the images would not come. And then I fell ill."

"But soon you will be well again. Are you good at solving conundrums, Sidonie Quince?"

"My lady?"

"My brother brought me a message. But he spoke in riddles, as they say the dead do."

"He spoke, my lady?"

"Nay, rather, he wrote." Mary Gilbert took something out of her pocket and held it out to Sidonie. It was a velvet-bound journal, richly decorated with pearls. A cold fist squeezed Sidonie's heart. She seen that journal before, in her fever-dream. And in that dream she had watched the shade of Sir Philip Sidney take up a pen, and write.

But, thought Sidonie, with a chill prickling along her spine, *the spirits who come to us in dreams leave no mark upon the waking world.*

"Read for yourself," said the Countess.

Sidonie opened the book, flipped through pages covered with Lady Mary's small neat script, and then stared at the words scrawled hastily across an empty sheet.

Quaere ubi pisces silentia servant.

Chapter Fifteen

Your answer, sir, is enigmatical.
— William Shakespeare, *Much Ado About Nothing*

Sidonie had managed this morning to eat a little stewed fruit and a morsel of manchet bread. When Kit looked in after an early ramble, she was sitting up in a fur-trimmed dressing-gown, a book open on her lap, gazing through the open window.

"Sidonie?"

She turned at the sound of his voice. He was flushed from his exercise, and brought with him an autumnal smell of woodsmoke.

"Kit. I have a riddle for you."

"I was never good at riddles," he reminded her.

Wordlessly she handed him a sheet of paper.

Kit read the copied Latin inscription and glanced up, bemused. "Seek where fish keep silence?"

"Yes. I know it sounds like nonsense, but that is the nature of riddles, is it not?"

"And who has posed this riddle?"

She hesitated, fearing Kit's skepticism, or worse, his laughter. Should she reveal a truth she scarcely believed herself? "It came to me in a fever-dream. I imagined I saw a wandering spirit, a ghost, and he wrote these words in a book."

Kit gave her a narrow look. "A message from the grave? Sidonie, do you believe in such things?"

"Mayhap I do. I know my father does. He spoke sometimes of necromancy — though mercifully he never dared to practise it. He said that ghosts know where treasure is hid, and can be summoned to reveal their secrets."

"Methinks if I were summoning ghosts, I would look for a plainer speaking one."

"Kit, you must not scoff. When the dead come to us in our dreams, they speak the language of dreams, and we needs must listen. Think, Kit. Where do fish keep silence?"

"Why, everywhere," said Kit. He added solemnly, "I believe it is one of the great virtues of fish."

"Pray be serious, Kit."

"Then tell me — where is silence kept?"

"In a convent," Sidonie said. "Or — she stared at Kit in sudden surmise — in a monastery! Surely it must mean Glastonbury. The treasure that was not accounted for — that Lady Mary believes was hidden by the monks."

"How then do you explain the fish?"

"I cannot explain the fish. But see, now at least we have half the message."

"If message it is," said Kit, "and not just a fever-fancy. But I must go — I have yet to break my fast." He smiled down at her as he took his leave. "You were always fonder of conundrums than I."

But, thought Sidonie, for Lady Mary, who had risked her immortal soul to summon her brother from the grave, this was no mere game of wits, no puzzle to fill an idle hour.

She, more than most, understood that the fate of England could hang on one galleon built with Glastonbury gold.

ॐ ॐ ॐ

In the afternoon Alice brought in a jug of mint tea, some almond cakes and a pot of citron marmalade — "nothing better to strengthen your stomach, mistress." As she poured the tea for Sidonie, she said, "Lady Mary would like to sit with you awhile, if you are well enough."

"But of course," said Sidonie. She was weary of her four bedroom walls and eager for company.

"I have good reports from Dr. Moffett," said the Countess, as she settled her heavy dark skirt around her. "He tells me your fever is quite gone."

"Entirely, my lady. Tomorrow, if the weather is warm, he says I may go sit in the garden for a little."

"Then perhaps I will join you. But in the meantime, I must ask — have you thought upon the words I showed you?" Though Lady Mary's gaze was level and serene, her hands, clasped in her lap, twisted nervously one upon the other.

"I have, my lady. And I think I have puzzled out a part of the riddle." Sidonie drew a long breath. "If in truth ghosts can show the way to hidden treasure, then you must seek at Glastonbury."

Lady Mary's broad, pale brow furrowed. "So we have always believed. But where, Sidonie? Treasure-hunters have sought out hidden passages, searched in the crypt beneath the Lady Chapel . . . all to no avail."

"I think," said Sidonie, "that Sir Philip has offered you the missing clue."

"But you cannot say where the gold is hidden?"

"Forgive me, my lady — I have half the solution, not the whole."

"But if you were to look into the crystal? Sidonie, will you scry for me again?"

"Scry, my lady? But I failed before."

"Surely this time you will succeed. My brother's message was meant for you, Sidonie."

Sidonie stared at her, dismayed. "That cannot be, my lady. It is you who binds him to this world, you who summoned him." She unfolded the paper she had shown Kit and held it out to the Countess. "See, he wrote the singular, *quaere*, as though for your eyes alone."

"Yes," said the Countess. "But he looked straight at you, Sidonie, as you stood in the doorway thinking you were unobserved."

"What must I do, my lady?"

"When you are strong again, I would have you go to Glastonbury. I have faith in your powers, Sidonie Quince. God does not ask more of us than we are capable of doing." Then, as though reading Sidonie's silence for refusal, she went on, "There is much at stake. While wars rage across Europe, while darkness surrounds us, Queen Elizabeth has given us prosperity and peace. We are fairly taxed, and lightly ruled. To be a subject nation, to see English streets awash with Protestant blood . . . under Spanish rule, Sidonie, have you thought what would become of you and me? Of all our kind?"

We would burn as witches, Sidonie answered silently.

She thought of the St. Bartholomew's Day Massacre — one more horror in a century of horrors, a tale kept alive by old men around the fire. The blood of countless innocent souls ran in the gutters of Antwerp and Paris, but

Sidonie could not weep for them. There were too many, they were faceless and nameless, for such enormity the task of grieving had no beginning and no end. You would go mad if you were to dwell on such things. You would go mad if you thought about the good and honourable men who lost their heads in King Henry's time, whose only crime was their stubborn faith; and if you imagined the torment of those who died in Mary's fires.

Sidonie grieved for her mother; that was as much sorrow as her heart could bear. Must she grieve also for the old monk who, faithful to his last breath, guarded the lost treasures of Glastonbury?

Chapter Sixteen

It is the bright day that brings forth the adder,
and that craves wary walking.
      — William Shakespeare, *Julius Caesar*

For their return to Glastonbury, Lady Mary lent them horses from her stables — a nimble white gelding for Kit, and for Sidonie, riding nervously sidesaddle, a placid chestnut mare. They set out on a day of hazy sunshine, clattering along the narrow road amid fields so intensely green that even now, in autumn, they seemed suffused with light. Sidonie remembered that in the days of Arthur's Camelot these were the flooded Summer Lands, and Glastonbury was Ynys-witrin, The Isle of Glass, a holy island encircled by lagoons and interlacing streams. Perhaps, she thought, it was those waters still lying close beneath the surface that kept the pasturelands so lush and green. Or was it the ancient magic that clung to Glastonbury's meadows like October mist?

ॐ ॐ ॐ

A chill wind blew among the ruins of the Abbey. Oak leaves, scattered across the paths, promised an early winter. They found the grounds deserted, save for a boy of twelve or so who half-dozed under a sunny wall while his flock grazed among the tumbled stones.

Lifting her skirts and treading carefully through the long wet grass, Sidonie approached the shepherd. "Have you seen the old monk who comes here?" she asked.

"Oh aye," said the boy, gazing up at her with sleepy eyes. "A fortnight ago, he drove my sheep out of the Lady Chapel. though they did no harm."

"But today?"

"Not today, mistress, nor I hope any day hereafter."

Sidonie felt a chill of premonition. "And why is that?"

"He died, mistress."

In the midst of surprise and sadness, Sidonie felt a half-guilty relief. Am I so wicked, she wondered, to think it a blessing, that the old man will never know what I have come to do?

"How came he to die?" she asked the boy.

"Why, in his bed, mistress. He was old, you see, and wore out from praying." The boy was wide awake now, and anxious to share his special knowledge. "He showed me a gold cross once, that he swore held a relic of Christ, a nail from the crucifixion. They say that the day before he died he crawled on his knees all the way up Wearyall Hill, dragging that cross behind him."

For Sidonie, relief gave way to a terrible pity. For what sin could God have demanded from that good old man such heavy penance? Or maybe it was not penance at all, but merely one more test of his life-long devotion.

The boy added, "When they found him dead, he still held the cross in his arms. There was a great argument as to what should become of it, for I think there are some in

the village who cling to the old faith, and they wanted him
buried with it."

"And was he?"

The boy shook his head and grinned. "Nay, mistress, it
was gold, you see, and studded with gems, and my father
thinks they took it away to Wells Cathedral."

"Perchance," asked Kit, strolling up behind them, "did
the old man raise fish?"

Sidonie guessed at once the reason for his question. If
the old monk had saved a gold cross from the Abbey, what
other treasure might he have hidden in his cottage garden?

The boy gave him a blank look. "Raise fish? Not that I
ever knew." He added helpfully, "There are fish aplenty in
the River Brue, all free for the taking."

Sidonie and Kit glanced at each other, sharing the same
thought. *Is there Abbey gold at the bottom of the River Brue?* But,
decided Sidonie, if the monks had thrown their treasures
into the river, what hope would they have of recovering it?

"Where fish keep silence," Sir Philip had written. Surely
he did not mean the river or the village. Aloud, she said,
"I remember no fish pond in the Abbey grounds."

"Is it the Abbey pond you mean?" said the shepherd.
"Why did you not say so before? Not enough fish in it now
to bother with — though I still see the little lads from the
village going up the path with their pails and nets."

"Prithee, will you show us the path?" asked Sidonie.

"It starts there, by the Abbey cloister." The lad gestured,
without getting up.

"Do you mind our horses, then," said Kit, and handed
him tuppence.

They found the way after some searching: an overgrown
footpath winding among ancient yews and hawthorn

thickets. They pushed through the tangle of brambles and hazel saplings that half-hid the entrance, and started single-file along the narrow track.

Sidonie, walking after Kit, stopped suddenly and half-turned. Was that rustling in the bracken only a fox, or something heavier-footed?

"What is it?" asked Kit, glancing back.

Sidonie shook her head, unable to explain the faint tingling on the nape of her neck that warned her they were not alone, that they were being watched.

"Sidonie, did you hear something?"

"No," she said. "It was nothing. Only I have these foolish fancies sometime, that someone is there, that there are eyes upon me."

Kit came back along the path, and they stood together, listening. There was nothing on the path behind them, no sound now but the wind stirring the leaves.

They went on a little further, and came to the edge of a large round pond. Beyond, to the north-east, they could see the Tor, with mist clinging to its slopes.

In the great days of the Abbey the pond must have been well kept and teeming with fish, but now the water, low at this time of year, was scummed with algae, fouled with rotting leaves. Rank grass and water weeds grew over the encircling wall of stones, and moss-furred tree limbs, felled by the wind, lay half-submerged among the lily pads. There was a rich damp smell of decaying vegetation.

Kit found a long branch and kneeling at the pond's edge, felt for the bottom. The stick sank deep.

"I've no mind to go wading in that," he remarked. "You must look into your scrying ball, Sidonie. If indeed there is gold down there, under fifty years or more of mud, the Countess will have to drain the pool."

Sidonie took the crystal from her pocket and laid it at the edge of the pool on its felt wrapping. The slanting afternoon sun filled the glass with shards of light. Turning away from the dazzle, Sidonie spoke her thoughts aloud. "Kit, are we mad, do you think?"

"No more than the rest of the world," replied Kit with good humour. He settled down on the grass beside her. "But why do you ask me that now?"

"Because I fear we are seeking a chimera — the phantasy of a wishful mind. Maybe there was never any hidden gold, or maybe it was discovered half a century ago. And we have strayed far from our purpose. Should we not collect more of the red elixir, and take it to my father so that he can make gold for the Queen?"

Kit said, with more than a hint of irony, "I applaud your faith in your father's skills." Sidonie answered him with a rueful smile.

Kit added, soberly, "Whatever we choose to do, Sidonie, we are chasing will o' the wisps. The red earth may be the alchemist's elixir — or it may be rust-coloured mud. There may be a fortune in gold at the bottom of the fish pond, or there may be nothing but weeds and kitchen refuse. But all things considered, your best chance of saving your father's neck from the noose is to present the Queen with Glastonbury gold."

"How sensible you are," sighed Sidonie. "Go then, see to the horses, and leave me do what I must." She watched as Kit disappeared down the Abbey path, and after a moment turned reluctantly back to the crystal.

The sun, now low on the horizon, was at the wrong angle, she decided, and she moved into the shade of a thorn tree. How to begin?

She tried to focus, conjuring up images of gold candlesticks, censers, chalices. Clouds swirled in the glass, hinted at shapes, dissolved into nothing.

Somewhere close by a twig snapped. "Kit?" she murmured, half in trance. There was no answer, only the faint sound of breathing.

The hair stirred on the back of her neck. She snatched up the crystal and thrust it into her pocket, then turned to look over her shoulder, her gaze meeting cold grey eyes under a wide-brimmed hat. Rough hands gripped her arms and twisted them behind her. A voice said, "An' you value your life, Mistress Quince, you will not cry out."

Chapter Seventeen

It is the treasure of treasures, the supreme philosophical potion, the divine secret of the ancients. Blessed is he that finds such a thing.
— The *Alchemical Mass* of Nicholas Melchior

Sidonie choked back a scream. What could he want with her, this grim-faced stranger who had stepped from the shadow of the trees? And how could he know her name? Before Sidonie had time to gather her wits, her hands were bound behind her, and a gag was thrust into her mouth so that she could not cry out. The harder she squirmed and struggled, the more the rope chafed her wrists. The sour taste of the rag in her mouth made her stomach heave.

Then he blindfolded her and tossed her like an awkward bundle over his shoulder. Through the loose-woven fabric across her eyes she had a sense that they were passing through shade, and sun, and then shade again. Sometimes tree branches brushed against her. They went down some steps, and crossed what she guessed, from the sound of the man's boots, was an uneven stone floor. Then abruptly she was set upon her feet.

"There is a knife at your ribs, mistress," the man cautioned her. "If you are wise, you will do exactly as I say."

Blood pounded in her ears; she could feel her heart drumming against her ribs.

"Stoop down," the man said. With one hand on the top of her head, the other at her waist, he guided her through some sort of low opening.

The air felt cold, and there was a dank smell of earth and stone. She stood quiet while her captor removed the gag from her mouth, the blindfold from her eyes. Still she could see nothing; a thick stale blackness pressed against her.

Presently a candle flared. In the wavering circle of its flame she saw a long, dour face, deeply furrowed at mouth and brow, framed by lank pale hair. A harsh face, with no hint of pity in it. Behind him was a rough stone wall, stretching away into darkness. She realized they were in a passageway or tunnel.

Her legs trembled; for a moment she feared they would give way. She drew a long shuddering breath. "Where are we?" she said. And then, when there was no answer, "What do you want with me?"

"Summat that will make me richer, and leave you no poorer," said the man, and in the flickering light he gave her a wolfish grin.

Sidonie's heart lurched. Her belly cramped with dread.

"I have naught to give you," she whispered, knowing full well she did, and praying that she mistook his intent.

"Come to that, you have what every woman has," he said. "Nay, don't flatter yourself, Mistress Quince, that's not what I need from you. Nor the gold in your purse, either." He reached up to set the candle in an iron sconce on the wall.

"We both have secrets, mistress. Mine is where to find this tunnel under Glastonbury; and yours is where to find the magic elixir that will change base metal into gold. Share your secret with me, and you will go free. Keep it, and I fear it must die with you in this unwholesome place."

"We found no elixir," Sidonie told him. "I have no more notion than you where it may be hid."

The anger in his face made her throat go dry. "Mistress, do not trifle with me. You are the daughter of an alchemist, and you have come to Glastonbury, where by Dr. Dee's own account he and Kelley found the Red Lion. Would you have me believe you came here for a lover's tryst? Or maybe to gather wormy apples in the Abbey orchard?"

"We came to visit the old monk, who had been kind to us. We did not know he was dead." She knew he could hear the terror in her voice. Her teeth were beginning to chatter, from cold as well as fright.

"So you say. But I know it for a pretext. Tell me no more lies, my girl. I know what you keep in your skirt pocket, and I know what a scryer does. Edward Kelley is a scryer, and it was he who found the alchemist's stone at Glastonbury."

"I cannot scry with my hands fastened," she said. For answer he moved behind her, and she felt him fumbling at her bonds. She pulled her hands free, shook the stiffness out of them.

She took the crystal from her pocket. There was nowhere to set it down, so she held it on her outstretched palm. "I need more light."

He lit another candle, raised it between them. "What do you see?"

"Prithee have patience. I must wait for the glass to clear."

She kept him waiting long enough for the candle to burn down, and he had to dig in his pack for another.

Finally, she said, "Lower the light a little." And then, "It may be that I see something."

She could feel his breath hot on her cheek as he leaned over her shoulder, trying to look into the crystal.

She turned her head, said irritably, "I can do nothing if you hang over me like that."

He mumbled something, and moved back.

"There," she said at last. "But I see no treasure. I see a tower."

"A tower?" he prompted her impatiently. "Is it the broken tower on the Tor?"

She shook her head. "I see a tower on a bridge. Methinks it is London Bridge."

He said, with a new note of menace in his voice, "Play no games with me, mistress. It is here the elixir is hid, not in London City."

"It is not the elixir I see. There is a kind of whimsy in this glass — like a flaw in the crystal. Sometimes, if it has a mind to obey, it reveals the thing you are seeking. But other times it shows the future, whether or not you wish to know it."

"Whose future, then?" She could sense, beneath his impatience and mistrust, a growing uncertainty.

"Why, England's, sometimes. Or it may show what lies ahead for the one who consults it. Like yourself."

She had him now. He said, "Mayhap it shows me returning to London with the elixir."

"Mayhap. If that were destined to happen. But that is not what the crystal shows."

"Then tell me."

"I see a tower on a bridge," she repeated. "And on that tower I see a head, impaled on a traitor's pole."

In the silence she could hear the sharp intake of his breath.

"Whose head?" he asked at last.

Sidonie turned away from the crystal, looked calmly into his eyes. "Yours," she said.

His mouth twisted. "The glass lies."

"Does it? Glastonbury belongs to the Crown, and so the elixir you wish to steal is the rightful property of the Queen. Whether you seek it for your own ends, or for the King of Spain, that makes you a thief and a traitor. It was one of your henchmen, was it not, who tricked my father into employing him, and so was privy to his secrets?" She took the man's silence for answer. "He must have read the message I left for my father, and told you where to find me. One of your agents followed me to the inn at Salisbury. Another attacked me on the road and stole my purse. My steps have been dogged every mile of the way. To me, that stinks of conspiracy."

He scowled down at her, jaw set, holding back his anger. He was a tall man, broad in the chest and shoulders. She could not hope to overpower him, though perhaps she could outrun him. But could she outwit him? Therein, she thought, lay her best hope. How many plots and conspiracies, how many threats to the throne had Good Queen Bess survived, through guile and deviousness? Elizabeth had never hesitated to use her women's weapons, and they had served her well. If Sidonie could not manage to defeat her enemies by simple cunning, then she was not as clever as her father believed.

"But what will you do with the elixir if you find it? Are you an alchemist, then?"

"There are those I know who practise the craft."

"Practise it, perhaps — but have they the knowledge to succeed, where so many have failed? Have you the knowledge to tell who is a charlatan, and who is not? Remember too, that no one can succeed in making gold unless he is of a pure and blameless heart. Surely if you obtain the elixir by force, all its power will be lost."

"You argue like a Jesuit," the man said. She could hear a certain grudging admiration in his voice.

"And," she said, seizing her slight advantage, "you have only the account of Dee and Kelley, that they found the elixir at Glastonbury. What profits them, to reveal such a secret to the world? Mayhap even now in Bohemia they are laughing up their sleeves, that they have sent so many English fools on a wild goose chase."

He half-raised his hand, and she winced away, fearing that he meant to strike her.

She said, quickly, "If I am to scry, I must have some reason to believe in what I do, some hope of success."

His hand had dropped to his side. She held her gaze steady under his cold, assessing stare. Did he realize that she was trying to buy time through sheer confusion?

Finally he said, "Very well, Mistress Quince. I will give you a reason to believe. Do you know the tale of Parzival?"

She nodded.

"So mayhap you recall these words. 'There is a stone of purest kind. By the power of that stone the phoenix burns to ashes, but the ashes give him life again. And such power does the stone give a man that flesh and bones are made young again. And the name of the stone is *lapsit exillis.*'"

He saw her puzzled look. "And I was told you were a scholar, Mistress Quince. That may sound dog Latin to you, but let me pronounce it otherwise. What means *lapis elixir*?"

"Elixir stone? You speak of the alchemist's elixir, the Red Lion?"

"Now you have it. But in the story of Parzival it is given another name, this substance that can turn the seas to molten gold, can bring the phoenix back to life, and give a man eternal youth. It is called the Holy Grail."

Sidonie gave a gasp of startled laughter. "You would have me believe that you are searching for the Grail? That the elixir and the Grail are one and the same? How can that be, when the Grail is the chalice of the Last Supper?"

"As some would have it," he said. "The chalice from which Christ drank, and which caught his blood as he hung on the cross. But the Grail is a mystery, holding secrets of which mortal man cannot conceive. Mysteries take many forms, so that their true nature may not be revealed to the unworthy. To some it may be a golden cup, a chalice . . . to others it may appear as a stone, no different from any stone at the side of the path."

Her father's words came back to Sidonie: *A stone, yet not a stone. A thing worthless, yet valuable beyond price; a thing unknown, yet known to everyone.* And she thought of the beggar who had attacked her on the road. When he looked into her purse, hoping to find the holiest of relics, and saw nothing but red mud, surely he must have thrown it away in disgust.

"And how can you be sure the Grail is at Glastonbury?"

"Because when Joseph of Arimathea, who was the first Keeper of the Grail, came to England, he planted his staff at Glastonbury; and the Angel Gabriel appeared to him, and commanded him to build a church. It is here, where England's first church stood, that the Grail is hidden."

"All this is the stuff of legend," Sidonie said.

"A legend that has endured because it is the truth."

Sidonie knew then that it was not for his own advantage, nor for the Spanish king's, that he risked a conspirator's death. What drove this man was religious zeal, blind dedication to an uncompromising belief. The Grail was the cup of the First Mass, that contained the life-blood of God. Its possession meant the power to unseat the Protestant Queen and restore England to the Old Faith.

He held her by her upper arms, fingers digging into the tender flesh. "The stone is here. In one guise or another, it is hidden at Glastonbury."

"I have it not," Sidonie said. "It is true, I wished to deceive you. I had the elixir once — the Grail, if that is what you wish to call it. But I have hidden it once again, where it will not easily be discovered."

"But you will tell me where it is."

"I could if I wished, but how would you know when you had it? One stone, amid these ruins, this waste of broken stone?"

"Because you will find it for me."

"Yes," Sidonie told him. "Show me the way out of this place, and I will find the stone. It is your only hope of possessing it."

He made no answer, but turned and walked toward the tunnel entrance. She heard him grunt with effort as he lifted the bar, and then hinges creaked as the door swung open. Grey light seeped in through a low archway. Her captor picked up the rope that had bound Sidonie's hands. He stared at her in a considering way, then tossed it aside.

As she emerged through the opening, Sidonie glanced round, and after a moment of disorientation, recognized the tiled floor of the crypt beneath the Lady Chapel. She and Kit had explored this place on their earlier visit — how had the tunnel entrance escaped their notice? Then she saw the reason. The archway had been doubly concealed by a rampant growth of ivy pushing through breaks in the wall, and by a shoulder-high pile of rubble and broken stones. Had her captor stumbled upon the tunnel by accident, she wondered, or had the secret been handed down to those who still held to the old faith?

The man bent down and drew the tangle of greenery like a curtain over the doorway. Then, straightening, he gave Sidonie a questioning look.

"I'll lead the way," she said; and he shrugged his assent.

As they left by the south door of the Lady Chapel, the last light was fading. Sidonie wondered, with rising panic, what Kit had thought when he returned to the fishpond and discovered her gone. If only he were waiting near the Abbey with the horses. He might hear if she cried out, and so would come to her aid. But she could catch no glimpse of him among the ruined archways, nor hear any sound of horses.

They moved in silence along the wooded pathway to the Tor. All the while Sidonie's thoughts were circling and darting, seeking some way to escape. She knew that this man would not willingly set her free; now that she understood so much, he could not let her live.

This was a problem to be solved like any other problem, she told herself; though a small insistent voice reminded her, *not quite like any other problem, when the wrong answer means your death.*

They had reached the bottom of the Pilgrim's Path that climbed the Tor to St. Michael's tower. Mist was rising from the cold, damp ground, swirling and billowing around them. In fog and darkness, Sidonie decided, lay her one chance of escape. She pointed upward through the gathering dusk.

"There," she said. "If the legends be true, then the Grail belongs both to our world, and to the Otherworld. What better hiding place, than where the two worlds meet?"

She turned away, and started purposefully up the path.

In ancient times, before St. Michael built his Christian church, the Tor was thought to be inhabited by older gods. There, so said the romances, lay the entrance to Annwyn, the Underworld; and there at the top of the haunted mountain Gwynn ap Nudd, Lord of the Underworld, had built his palace. Indeed, thought Sidonie, as the chill grey mist enfolded her, it was as though with every step they were ascending farther away from the mortal world, and closer to the world of faerie. She wondered, when St. Michael's church was rent asunder, had the pagan gods returned? Did Gwynn ap Nudd and his red-eyed hounds once again ride out in the Wild Hunt, summoning the souls of the dead?

Her soul, if she could not outwit this grim-faced man who walked behind her. She shivered, and drew her cloak close round her.

They came to the top of the Tor, and the broken tower. The mist roiled round them, hiding the woods and fields below them, obscuring the path they had followed. Her captor's face was a featureless blur in the grey gloom. "Hurry," he said. "Night is almost upon us. Give me the stone."

"Do you be patient," said Sidonie. "I will fetch it. Have you a candle with you, and the means to light it?"

She saw him fumbling in his pouch, heard him curse as he dropped his flint and bent to retrieve it. And then she was running, blindly, recklessly, faster than she had ever run before, faster than she had imagined possible; holding her skirts high as she raced for her life down the shrouded slopes of the Tor.

Chapter Eighteen

Sable night, mother of dread and fear.
— William Shakespeare, *The Rape of Lucrece.*

More than once in that headlong flight she stumbled, grazing her hands and knees as she fell, each time picking herself up with desperate haste. Then abruptly she was on level, wooded ground. Through fog-shrouded trees she could see the dim outlines of the Abbey buildings.

She heard a rattle of loose stones behind her, and a muffled curse. She ran faster, thorn branches clutching at her garments. There was a stitch in her side, and her chest hurt. She knew that her pursuer was gaining ground; but where could she find a hiding place in these ruins, with all their roofs and windows open to the night?

And then she remembered the tunnel beneath the Lady Chapel, with its heavy oaken door. There was refuge there, if only she could reach it.

Her breath came in painful gasps as she raced along the path and down the stairs to the crypt beneath the Lady Chapel. She tore aside the curtain of ivy, pushed open the tunnel door and ducked under the lintel. Then she closed the door behind her and dropped the bar.

Almost at once she heard the clatter of the outer latch. Panicked, she fled along the passageway, feeling her way in the darkness with one hand against the tunnel wall. In her haste she stumbled, almost losing her balance, as her foot skidded in a patch of something slick and wet.

Tunnels were meant to lead somewhere. Over the centuries many feet must have trod these flagstones, on who knew what secret assignations. But the monks had been gone for fifty years. By now the passage could be blocked with rubble, or the exit walled up with bricks. She could be trapped here for hours, or days, until her pursuer gave up the chase.

Now she could hear something heavy thudding against the door. She reminded herself that the boards were thick, the hinges sturdy. One man, working alone, would be hard put to batter it down.

As a child, walking abroad with her father, she had loved the dark, had been excited by it; but then there had been stars and moon overhead, a lamp in her father's hand, glints of candlelight through shuttered windows. This was the darkness of the tomb, stifling and oppressive; the formless, featureless dark of the alchemist's *nigredo*. It had weight and substance as it pressed against her eyes, her mouth; she drew it into her lungs with every breath.

The thudding had stopped. All she could hear now were her own footsteps on the paving stones, and somewhere ahead, a slow tap, tap of water dripping. Step by step she moved forward, one hand tracing the tunnel wall. The passage, which at first had been wide enough for two to walk abreast, grew narrower, so that she could touch the two sides with her outstretched hands. And then, with dismay, she found her shoulders brushing against the stones on either side. What if the walls met, and there was no way through? She sensed as well that the roof was pressing down on her, and she tried not think of the massive weight of earth and stone overhead.

She dared not go back; there was no choice but to push forward. The roof, now, was so low that she could no longer walk erect, but must drop to her hands and knees.

She bundled up her skirts as best she could and tucked them into her girdle. For what seemed like hours she inched her way along the rough flagstones. Her stockings were shredded, her knees scraped raw. Her face was covered with cold sweat.

And then she could go no farther. Her mouth went dry, her throat constricted as she realized she had come to a solid brick wall.

A part of Sidonie, at that moment, wanted to give way to despair, to throw herself down and weep with anger and sheer frustration. But she had to reckon with that other part of herself, that would not give up on a problem until she had exhausted every means to solve it. And so she ran her hands slowly along the top of the wall, and down the sides, and across the middle, in the hope of finding crumbled mortar, a brick she could work loose, some means of opening a way through. Then, as she crouched on her heels, her hand encountered a wedge-shaped brick. She felt to one side and then the other, and realised that it was the keystone of an arch.

The opening, set low down in the wall, was not large, but there was room enough for her to squeeze through. She gathered her skirts around her, and crept through to the other side.

ॐ ॐ ॐ

A smell of dust and mildew prickled her nostrils. Close by, something scratched and scrabbled — rats, she thought with a shudder. Faintly, from above, came the sound of music. Groping in the dark, she discovered a row of casks, an overturned bench or table — and then a stair-rail. Holding tight to the rail she climbed a narrow flight of stairs towards a sliver of yellow light. At the top she found hinges, a latch.

Pray God, she thought, *that there is no one on the other side who means me harm.* She tried the latch, but the door would not open. She shouted, and hammered her fists on the wood. She heard someone call out in a startled voice. More voices joined in. There were hurried footsteps, and then the door swung open.

She wavered for a moment on the sill, squinting into a long, low-ceilinged, smoky room, filled with the flickering glow of rushlights. And then her strength failed her. She swayed, tottered, and collapsed into the bewildered grasp of a large, red-bearded man.

"God's mercy, what have we here?" the man said. He held Sidonie at arms length, examining her with curiosity and mild alarm.

All at once there were a dozen people jostling for a better view. Someone offered helpfully, "Methinks 'tis a wench."

"I can see that, plain enough," said red-beard. "But how came she into my cellar?"

"Through the tunnel from the Abbey, like as not." An old man's voice, raspy and querulous. "Had a sheep do that once. No young maids, though, nor any monks since King Henry's time."

Dazedly, Sidonie looked round — it seemed she was at an inn, or an ale-house. There was a babble of voices, faces crowding close.

Just then a sturdy young woman in a homespun gown pushed through the crowd. Her broad, fair face was flushed with indignation. "Fie, for shame," she scolded. "Away with your questions, leave the poor maid be, can't you see what a state she is in, all smutched and draggled?"

Sidonie could only imagine what a tatterdemallion she must look. She had long since lost her cap and there was a rip in her cloak where it had caught on a thorn bush. Her shoes and the hem of her skirt were caked with mud. Distractedly she raised one hand to smooth down the wild tangle of her hair. "Prithee," she said, "what place is this?"

"Why, 'tis the Pilgrims' Inn. My father is the innkeeper. And you'll be the lass that's gone missing, I'll warrant. Your lad was here earlier, all in a fret and asking after you. How you came to be in that cellar, I cannot fathom."

"Nor I," said Sidonie. She might have invented a story, but she was too weary to try.

"Come sit by the hearth," said the woman. "There's a kettle of pottage on the fire. Are you hungry?"

Sidonie nodded, realising suddenly that she was famished. Her legs felt weak, from exhaustion and sheer relief. She was safe, for now, in the midst of these good-humoured, inquisitive country folk. But where was Kit?

She drew up a bench and huddled close to the fire. Presently the woman brought her a bowl of stew and a tankard of mulled ale. The ale was steaming hot and heavily spiced. The first few sips sent a flush of warmth to Sidonie's face.

She blew on her stew to cool it. "But where is he now, my young man?"

"Why, he has gone with the village lads to scour the Abbey ruins for you."

"Will you send after him, then, and say I am here, and quite safe withal?"

"Never fear, " said the innkeeper's daughter. "My father has already sent the stableboy."

ॐ ॐ ॐ

"What a fright you gave me when I found you gone, Sidonie Quince!" Kit had seized hold of her hand, and seemed loathe to let it go. "And when I asked the shepherd lad, he offered me small comfort. He supposed you had been carried down to Annwn by the King of Faerie."

Sidonie summoned the ghost of a smile, and left her hand in Kit's warm grasp. "Mayhap," she said, "that was the truth of it, Kit — I was stolen by Gwynn ap Nudd, and all this while I have been wandering in the Underworld."

CHAPTER NINETEEN

Foul-cankering rust the hidden treasure frets,
But gold that's put to use more gold begets.
— William Shakespeare, *Venus and Adonis*

The innkeeper had sent a messenger ahead to Wilton House, and next day at midmorning Adrian Gilbert arrived in person to collect Kit and Sidonie. After a good night's sleep and an early breakfast of yesterday's bread and cold roast mutton, Sidonie's spirits had risen a little. Nonetheless she had two skinned knees and sundry scrapes and bruises to remind her of last night's misadventure. As they rode across the fields in bright autumn sunshine, her mind was on hot baths, rose-scented soaps and Alice's cheerful ministrations.

"It seems, Mistress Quince," said Gilbert, riding abreast, "that you are oft in need of rescuing."

"Pray do not mock, Master Gilbert. He meant to kill me, if I did not do his bidding."

"I should never have left you alone," Kit said morosely. "The fault would have been mine, if harm had come to you."

"It was your fault least of anyone's," protested Sidonie. "How could you have guessed that such a peaceful place could harbour danger?"

"In these times," said Adrian Gilbert, "no place is peaceful. There are none of us safe. You least of all, when men believe that you hold the key to riches and power."

"Did I not tell you it was a curse?" said Sidonie. "And if I truly had foreknowledge . . . " She broke off, surprised by her own words. Suppose the power of foresight was not in her at all, but only in the crystal? So often her scrying produced a murky vision that try as she might, would not come clear.

Gilbert finished the thought for her. "With foreknowledge you would have known what lay ahead? Methinks, Sidonie, that you have the gift— or curse if you like — but it frightens you so much, that you will not give in to it."

Kit said, with a wry glance at Sidonie, "When you know her better you will realize she does not give in to anything."

Gilbert laughed. "'Struth, Kit, I am beginning to understand that."

Sidonie felt that she should defend herself. "In any case, it would have done no good to give in to the man who attacked me. In the end, it was not gold he wanted, but a thing beyond anyone's power to grant him."

"And pray what was that?"

"What only a madman would demand. He believed I could find the Holy Grail."

"Sidonie," said Gilbert, "you are ill-suited to living in this age. You lack fanaticism. Your curse is not foresight, but rather the curse of all mathematicians —a rational mind."

ॐ ॐ ॐ

That afternoon Sidonie, scrubbed and tidied and freshly gowned, walked with the Countess along the intricately twining pathways of the knot garden. The crisp air had put a little colour in Lady Mary's cheeks. Her step was brisk, and there was a new vigour in her voice.

"Will you look into the glass again, Sidonie? To dredge the pond will be no small task, but well worth the expense if my brother's message proves true."

Sidonie's stomach tightened. With a conscious effort she kept her voice steady. "My lady, do you mean me to return to Glastonbury?"

"My child," exclaimed Lady Mary, "do you imagine I would put you in such danger a second time? I never should have sent you and Master Aubrey off without an escort. I imagined the two of you travelling alone would escape attention, but foolishly, I did not weigh the risk." Absently, she bent to snap a faded marigold head. "You can scry at a distance, can you not?"

"I have done so, my lady."

"Then will you come to the library after dinner?"

"I will, my lady," said Sidonie with sinking heart.

ॐ ॐ ॐ

In the library the curtains had been drawn, the candles lit, the table prepared for her as before. Sidonie set the scrying crystal in the precise centre of the red silk cloth, and slowly willed her mind to stillness. This time, come what might, she was determined to succeed.

She thought of the terror and outrage she had felt at the hands of her captor. And she remembered Lady Mary's words: "Have you thought what would become of you and me, of all our kind, under Spanish rule?"

Always, she had been ready to see both sides of a question, to feel sympathy for the victims, whatever the cause. But this man who would deliver England into the hands of her enemies, who would have killed Sidonie in cold blood, without a second thought — what sympathy did he or his cause deserve?

The edges of her vision grew blurred as she focussed intently on the point of reflected light in the centre of the glass.

Never before had she felt such perfect quietude of mind. She realized, with vague astonishment, that there was no longer any holding back, no fear of what the crystal might reveal. To look into the glass and discover what was hidden could arm her with foreknowledge, but it changed nothing. Her mother had cheated fate by choosing the manner of her death, but she could not cheat death itself. The glass had revealed a truth as immutable as an algebraic solution.

Sidonie decided, at that moment, that her scrying was neither curse nor gift. She had no power to change what was foreordained. She possessed a skill, like any other — a skill that might well save her father's life, and help to save Elizabeth's throne.

She let her mind's eye linger on remembered images — the stagnant surface of the pond, fouled with rotting weeds, the mossy stones that encircled it, the trees beyond. Today the vision came sharp and clear. Unconsciously she sucked in her breath as dark water closed over her. Down and down she went, to where glints of gold showed through a blanket of black mud, hinting at what lay beneath. And as she went deeper still, in the heart of the crystal there appeared a glorious vision of censers and candlesticks and gold plate, of jewel-encrusted golden chalices: Abbey treasures hidden from the world for half a century.

Sidonie let out a long, slow breath. The image was quickly fading, but she had seen enough. This time she trusted, without question, her own gift, and the truth of what she had seen.

"Alice," she called out, and Alice put her head round the door so quickly that Sidonie guessed she had been waiting on the other side.

"Mistress?"

"Where is Lady Mary?"

"At her prayers, mistress."

"When she has finished, will you go to her and say that what was lost is found?"

Alice gave her a puzzled look. "What was lost . . . ?"

"Just say that, Alice. Nothing more. She will understand."

ॐ ॐ ॐ

Next morning Adrian Gilbert prepared to depart for Glastonbury with a work party and half a dozen armed guards. Sidonie came down to the courtyard to watch the men loading the wagon with tools and supplies.

"Let me come with you," she said to Gilbert, on the impulse of the moment.

Gilbert laughed. "And camp out for a week with the workmen? I doubt Lady Mary would countenance that."

And do you think me such a cossetted maid, that I have never slept rough? thought Sidonie; but out of politeness she held her tongue.

"Nay, Mistress Sidonie," said Gilbert, "you have done the best part of the work — the glory is all yours. What follows now is mere drudgery."

"I could stay at the Pilgrim's Inn," Sidonie pointed out. "I would think it a great favour, to be there when the treasure is found."

"Then so you shall be," said Gilbert, relenting. "I will send word when the pond is drained and the dredging begins, so that you and Master Aubrey may ride post haste to Glastonbury."

That week passed slowly for Sidonie, but at length the summons came, and she set out with Kit for Glastonbury in the mists of an October dawn. They found Adrian Gilbert knee-deep in mud at the pond's shallow margin. Climbing out, he waved them a cheerful greeting and squelched his way across the trampled grass.

"By the end of the first day's work," he told them, "I had lost all trust in visions. Even yours, Mistress Sidonie. But this morning, with the pool drained at last, we sank an iron-tipped pole into fifty years of muck and weeds and rubble, and struck what we think is metal."

Sidonie watched anxiously as the workmen dragged the morass at the pond-bottom with hooked poles and iron-clawed grapnels. Her heart leaped when one of them gave a great shout: "Master Gilbert, I have snagged summat!"

Everyone stopped to watch as the man heaved mightily on his pole, and succeeded in hauling a large weed-entangled object onto the grass. Adrian Gilbert raced to the spot with a bucket of clean water to flush away the mud.

Then a groan went up from the onlookers, and Gilbert turned to Sidonie with an apologetic grin. The treasure they had dragged with so much effort from the pond was a pot-metal cauldron with its side stoved in — no doubt a reject from the monastic scullery.

Sidonie stared down at it, a great ache of shame and disappointment swelling in her throat. *I am my father's daughter indeed,* she thought. *How else could I have put such foolish trust in shadows?*

Kit had come to stand beside her. His hand gripped hers. Sidonie looked up at him, blinking back tears. "How can they forgive me," she whispered, "for sending them on such a fool's errand?"

"Sidonie," said Kit, "has the glass ever yet played you false? Look there!"

And Sidonie watched with held breath as another workman freed a muddy cup-shaped object from the claws of the grapnel and rubbed his sleeve across it, leaving a wide, gleaming streak of gold.

ॐ ॐ ॐ

In fading afternoon light the Glastonbury treasures lay spread across the grass. Mud-spattered and exultant, Adrian Gilbert told Sidonie, "Once it's all cleaned and assessed we'll know better what we have. Still, I'll warrant it will buy our good Queen Bess a galleon or two."

Glinting yellow under a coating of mud and pond slime were chalices, candlesticks, plate, jewelled reliquaries, chests full of coins — gold to build ships for the Queen, to preserve her sovereignty over the seas, to keep England at peace. And gold to keep Sidonie's father safe from harm.

CHAPTER TWENTY

. . . with a monarch's voice,
Cry 'Havoc!' and let slip the dogs of war.
— William Shakespeare, *Julius Caesar*

"Mistress Quince, such news!" Alice was fairly dancing with excitement. Sidonie sat up in bed and reached for her dressing gown. There was an wintry chill in the room this morning.

"Tell me, Alice, I pray you, before you burst."

Alice set down the breakfast tray. "The word is all round the estate this morning, Mistress Sidonie. I have it from one of the cooks, who had it from the butler, who had it from the steward, who has it from Lady Mary's waiting-woman. The Queen herself is to come to Wilton House! If the weather holds she will be here in a fortnight!"

"So late in the year?" asked Sidonie, around a mouthful of bread and honey.

"Oh, but the Queen has long promised to pay another visit to Wilton House. Lady Mary was once at court, and Lady Mary's mother nursed Her Majesty through the pox, at much risk to her own life, so you see the Queen has much affection for the family, and the steward says that by next summer we may be at war with Spain, and then Her Majesty must bide in London . . . "

"Softly, softly, Alice," said Sidonie. She took a sip of hot milk. "If you go on at such a pace you will run out of breath entirely."

But Alice was not to be subdued. "My mother was a chambermaid," she chattered on, "when the Queen's Progress came to Wilton House, and she speaks of it still. Queen Elizabeth came with four hundred six-horse wagons to carry all the beds and furniture for her retinue, and five hundred officers and servants in her train. All the master's gentlemen and servants were lined up in the gatehouse courtyard thick as could be, and when the Queen arrived there was a great noise of guns fired off in salute, and then Lady Mary came out with all her divers ladies and gentlemen to greet the Queen."

Talking all the while, she fetched Sidonie a clean smock and underbodice and dropped a pair of lace-trimmed petticoats over her head. "What a time that was, my mother said, with the whole household turned topsy-turvy for months, cleaning and polishing and airing to get ready for the visit, and then the laying in of supplies, and hiring musicians, and borrowing Turkey carpets and extra silver plate from other houses. And then every day there were banquets and masques and entertainments, and hunting, and boating on the river, and fireworks at night."

Sidonie sat on the edge of the bed to pull on her stockings. "And for this visit, as well?" she asked with some alarm.

"Alas, no," sighed Alice, "as you point out, it is late in the year, and they say in the kitchen it is to be a modest affair, to spare expense to our house, and the Queen's coffers as well . . . " She threw open the wardrobe doors and peered inside. "No doubt," she observed, as she gathered up a set of embroidered sleeves and a kirtle of heavy russet silk, "Lady Mary will have more to tell you, for when you have broken your fast she awaits you in her parlour."

Sidonie found the Countess sitting in a high-backed chair with her prayer book in her lap, a piece of needlework spilling across a table at her side. The early sun, flooding through stained glass windows, scattered shards of emerald-green and vermilion across the rushmats.

"My dear Sidonie, come in. I have some news for you. You will have heard, I'm sure, that we were to expect a visit from the Queen."

"Alice mentioned something of the sort," said Sidonie, with tactful understatement.

"I have no doubt," said Lady Mary with a faint smile. "I understand Her Majesty wished to take possession of the Abbey treasure, and express her gratitude in person. However, word came this morning that she has been unwell, and her physicians have advised her not to travel."

"It is nothing serious, I hope?"

"A minor indisposition, we are told. But needless to say, it is disappointing."

"Indeed," said Sidonie — though in truth, Lady Mary seemed more relieved than disappointed.

"The real reason, I suspect, is not ill health, but rumour of an imminent attack by Spain. It's no secret that all shipping has been stayed, and the fleet fully mobilized."

Sidonie felt a chill at those words, so matter-of-factly spoken. On this tranquil October morning, with a lark outside the window and the sound of shepherd's pipes across the fields, could war be so near at hand? These past months all of England had held its breath, waiting for the Spanish ships, yet Sidonie still was unprepared.

"You have turned quite pale, my child. Forgive me, have I frightened you?"

"A little," Sidonie said.

The Countess reached for Sidonie's hand and held it in a firm, warm grasp. "Be of good heart, Sidonie. War is coming, none but a fool would deny it. But if Philip does not launch his ships before winter closes in, he needs must wait till spring. And remember this: the English fleet still rules the seas. Plymouth and London are filled with English fighting men, eager for the first sight of Spanish sails."

But Sidonie was only half attending to those brave words. "My lady, if there is to be war, I should be at home with my father, someone must see to his safety . . . "

Lady Mary's brows lifted. "And should he not instead be seeing to your safety?"

Sidonie hesitated, at a loss to explain, but Lady Mary seemed content to let the question rest.

"Sidonie, I did not send for you to speak of war, but only to say this: though the Queen must bide in London, we are nonetheless to entertain a distinguished visitor. Her Majesty is sending Lord Burleigh to fetch the gold, and he has asked to speak with you."

"What, I, my lady?" said Sidonie, flustered, her mind still elsewhere.

"And does that surprise you?" Lady Mary's voice was amused. "It is you who have earned the Queen's gratitude, you who have helped protect her throne. Have you so soon forgotten the prophecy — that when the Abbey treasure is discovered, peace will be assured in England?"

But Sidonie was remembering that other, darker prophecy of Regiomontanus: of catastrophe and ruin, of empires crumbling and lamentation across the land.

Chapter Twenty-One

The corners and straits of the earth shall be measured in depth. And strange shall be the wonders that are creeping into new worlds. Time shall be altered, with the difference of day and night.

— The spirit Madimi, to Doctor John Dee.

The day had dawned wet and blustery. Kit was in the library exploring the Earl of Pembroke's rare botanical texts, and after one glance at the drenched gardens, Sidonie decided to take her exercise in the Long Gallery. Seemingly unoccupied now that the gold had been recovered, Adrian Gilbert came to join her. Though fires had been lit at either end of the room the air was chilly, and they kept up a brisk pace as they marched the length of the gallery and back.

Gilbert appeared in high spirits after the success of his Glastonbury expedition.

"It was a happy stroke of fate that brought you to Wilton House," he told Sidonie.

Not so happy at first, thought Sidonie, remembering the cruel blow to Kit's head and her own terror, at the hands of the Counterfeit Crank. Still, she smiled in polite agreement.

"But perhaps not altogether an accident? You have not told me what it was you lost, on the road to Salisbury."

Sidonie hesitated. What *had* she lost? The red elixir —
or a handful of mud?

"Nay, you need not tell me, I have put together the
halves of the equation. An alchemist is employed by the
Queen to make gold for her coffers. His daughter, in the
face of all wisdom and common sense, makes a journey to
Glastonbury. It is no secret what Dr. Dee and his cohort
Edward Kelley claim to have discovered in the Abbey
ruins."

"All that is true enough," Sidonie admitted. "I greatly
feared for my father's life, if he could not fulfill his contract.
When I went to the scrying glass for help it showed me a
vision of Glastonbury. Then I thought I had found Dr.
Dee's elixir, but in the end it came to naught."

"But the glass did not lie, it was only that you misinter-
preted its message. The Queen has her gold — you have
fulfilled your father's obligation."

They came to the end of the gallery, turned and
retraced their steps. "You needs must have more faith in
your talent, Mistress Quince. The world is full of mountebanks who would deceive us with their tricks. And you, who
have the true God-given gift of vision, choose to hide your
light under a bushel. Would I had known of you five years
earlier."

Wherefore this talk of mountebanks? wondered Sidonie
in sudden alarm. Surely he did not speak of her father?
"What mean you, Master Gilbert?"

"Are you a patient listener, Mistress Quince? It is a tale
long in the telling."

Rain lashed the roofs of Wilton House; a rising gale
howled round the walls. "Since we are housebound," said
Sidonie, "it seems as good a way to pass the time, as any

other. Come, let us sit." She gestured to a cushioned bench close the by fire.

"So then," said Gilbert obligingly. "Imagine a seance at Mortlake, in the library of the famous Dr. Dee. There am I, with my good friend, the navigator John Davis. Sir Francis Walsingham by chance is there also. The arch-wizard Dr. Dee is in attendance, along with that lopped-eared charlatan Edward Kelley."

"Lopped-eared?" interrupted Sidonie.

"He had his ears cut off — they say for communicating with graveyard ghosts."

"Mercy!" said Sidonie with a shiver. "But do you continue, Master Gilbert."

"Kelley is kneeling in front of his scrying crystal, while Dee in his chair looks on. And then Kelley tells us that an angel spirit he calls "Madimi" has emerged from the crystal, bearing prophecies. But only Kelley can see and hear this chimera, and Dee must translate her words, for she speaks only in Greek, Arabic or Syrian."

"Indeed!" said Sidonie, stifling an urge to laugh. "And pray tell what prognostications did this apparition make?"

"Well, it may be that something was lost in the translation. But she spoke of strange wonders in new worlds, where time itself was altered, and of a northwest passage that would take us to Cathay. 'Let darkness go behind thee,' she was supposed to have said — and according to Dee, this signified the Midnight Sun."

"The polar sun, that in summer never sets?"

"The very one. And on the strength of these predictions, John Davis and I laid plans to mount a new expedition in search of this passage, in partnership with Dr. Dee. He named our little company "Colleagues or Fellowship of New Navigations Atlantical and Septentrional."

"A name to conjure with," observed Sidonie.

"Indeed. And it was Dee's conjuring that deceived us. John Davis is a brave and virtuous man, a peerless navigator, and my dearest friend; but the very sweetness of his nature made him gullible. As I was also, to my great regret. We knew John Dee as a mathematician and geographer, mapmaker to the Queen. And so we trusted him when he drew up a chart dictated by the spirit angel — though it showed that to reach Cathay we must cross a polar region of infinite ice."

"Marry, but this is a strange tale, Master Gilbert."

"And it grows stranger still. To my brother Humphrey, who like us had fallen under the wizard's spell, Dee had given a map that showed a great river cutting straight across the New World to the western ocean, from whence he could sail to Cathay. In gratitude, my brother granted Dee the rights to all lands in the New World north of fifty degrees. And then Dee came forward with a shipwrecked sailor, who spoke of lands in the New World with elephants and pepper trees, trees that poured forth wine, broad streets lined with silver mansions, gold nuggets as big as eggs in every stream, and savage kings bedecked with precious jewels.

"And so it was that my brother Humphrey set sail in a raging gale from Plymouth harbour, with five ships carrying carpenters, masons, smiths and sundry tradesmen, as well as musicians and Morris dancers to entertain the savage kings. Three of the ships survived to reach the Land of Cod, where they found a pleasant land of green grass and verdant woods."

"But no silver mansions, or savage kings?"

"None that were recorded. Though there were fish beyond number in the seas. It appears that, thus encouraged, my bold-hearted brother set off southward in search of the great river that would take him to Cathay.

"Alas, Mistress Quince, that river has proved as much a phantom as the spirit Madimi. Humphrey's venture ended, as you well know, in disaster. John Davis has just returned from the last of three long and perilous voyages to the New World; but he has never discovered the passage to Cathay. And when, as rumour has it, the spirit in Kelley's crystal, more strumpet than angel, began to make rude suggestions, Dee and Kelley set off on a tour of the royal houses of Europe, where they remain to this day."

And that, thought Sidonie, *is why my father is alchemist to the Queen, and why I am in Wilton House, wearing lace and velvet, instead of in Charing Cross, stirring pottage over the fire.*

Hard on the heels of that thought came another. There was much to do in Charing Cross, to ready the cottage for winter. And surely Emma and Sidonie's father, fending for themselves, would by now have driven one another to distraction. It was past time that she went home.

CHAPTER TWENTY-TWO

Never weather-beaten sail more willing bent to shore,
Never tired pilgrim's limbs affected slumber more.
  — Thomas Campion, *Two Books of Airs*

Lord Burleigh had arrived at Wilton House with little
fanfare. When Sidonie was summoned to his presence she
found him absorbed in a book, but now he marked the
place with a ribbon and set it aside.

"You sent for me, my lord?"

"Mistress Quince, how pleasant to see you again. I pray
you take a seat."

Sidonie sat gingerly on the edge of a damask-covered
chair.

Burleigh nodded toward the leather-bound volume on
the table. "Do you read Cicero, mistress?"

"I fear I do not, my lord. Affairs of state are quite beyond
my ken."

Burleigh smiled, and all at once Sidonie felt more at
ease. Lord of the Realm he might be, and confidant of the
Queen, but this grave, grey-bearded man in his sober black
gown seemed more scholar than courtier.

"All the same, you have performed no small service for
your country, Mistress Quince. Her Majesty wishes me to
convey her gratitude."

"You are kind to tell me so, my lord."

"And she would have you attend her at court, so that she herself may thank you."

"At court?" Sidonie was thrown suddenly into confusion. "My Lord Burleigh, do not think me insensible of this honour. But I have been long away from my father, and I needs must return to Charing Cross to see how he fares."

"Nay, Mistress Sidonie, be not alarmed, the Queen does not expect you to ride post haste to London. In any event," he added with a hint of irony, "at the moment she is herself much occupied with other matters. Do you go home, see to your own affairs, and in due course I will arrange for an invitation to be sent."

The knot in Sidonie's stomach loosened. Far too much had happened to her of late. She was weary of obligation, of protocol and ceremony; weary of life in this great house, in spite of all its comforts. She longed for her own bed, her own hearthfire. She needed to tend her garden, which by now must be in even worse disrepair, and harvest its fruits for winter. She longed even for the dull housewifely tasks that had once seemed mere distraction from her studies.

"Thank you, my lord," she said, dipping a half-curtsey; and gratefully made her escape.

ॐ ॐ ॐ

Sidonie drew her cloak close round her as she walked with Kit that afternoon through the Wilton gardens. It was a day of gathering cloud and fitful sunlight. A chill wind rattled through the branches of the ornamental trees. They crossed the deserted bowling green and wandered into the topiary garden, lingering among the artfully clipped shapes of elephants and peacocks.

"Mayhap you will be invited to the Accession Day tilts," said Kit. "That is a great occasion . . . I went once with my father, who had business in Westminster, and when we found ourselves outside Whitehall on Accession Day, Father made up his mind to spend the two shillings for places in the stands. 'Though it costs two day's earnings,' he said, 'it is such a sight as few men see in a lifetime.'"

"And was it so?" asked Sidonie.

"It was like nothing I had ever imagined — like a gorgeous dream," Kit said. "The nobles and the gentlemen of the court, dressed in glittering armour, made their entrance in carriages drawn by camels, and lions, and elephants . . . "

"Real ones? Truly?" interrupted Sidonie.

"Well, perhaps not," Kit conceded, "I think they may have been horses in disguise, but they were marvellous true to life. But to continue . . . All the servants and lance-bearers were dressed as savages from the Isles of Spice. And there was much sounding of trumpets, and lively music, and a great many romantic speeches addressed to the Queen, who watched with her ladies from a palace window . . . "

Anxious though Sidonie might be to return to the peaceful life of Charing Cross, to her books and her garden, she felt a flutter of excitement. The life of the palaces and great houses was an exotic otherworld of make-believe, of masques and plays and pageantry, a constant round of pleasure that common folk could scarce imagine. Wilton House had offered her a fleeting taste of that enchanted world. And who, having once visited it, would not wish to return?

"Lord Burleigh mentioned nothing of Accession Day," she said, a trifle wistfully, "and the seventeenth of November is not so very far off. Perhaps there will be a message waiting at my father's house?"

"Very possibly," said Kit; though she thought he looked a little apologetic, in case he had raised false hopes.

ॐ ॐ ॐ

On the eve of her departure, making her farewells, Sidonie sought out Adrian Gilbert. She found him in the physic garden, helping to prepare the beds for winter. Now that the rampant summer growth had died back she could better observe the harmonious ordering of the garden: four brick-edged squares enclosed in a circle, filled with medicinal plants from the four quarters of the globe.

Seeing Sidonie, Gilbert set down his spade, swept off his hat and made an extravagant bow. Sidonie smiled at this courtly greeting, so at odds with his rough workman's garb.

"Mistress Quince, I am sorry indeed to hear that you intend to leave us."

"In truth, Master Gilbert, I never meant to bide so long."

"Still, a pity you cannot be here for the yuletide. I mean us to have mummers, and masques, and music, and all manner of entertainments. Wilton House has been too long in mourning."

Sidonie smiled. Students of the occult, in her experience, were much like her father, thin and stooped and pale from crouching over dusty volumes in dim lit rooms. Yet this hale, broad shouldered, ruddy man embraced life with a rare exuberance. It was easy to imagine him as the Lord of Misrule, presiding with boisterous good humour over the Twelfth Night revels. Why, it occurred to Sidonie to wonder, had he never married? Had he perhaps decided that marriage and metaphysics were an uneasy mix? As for Sidonie, life with Simon Quince had thoroughly discouraged her from any thought of marrying an occultist.

ॐ ॐ ॐ

Lady Mary came out to the gates to see them off. Today she had given up her mourning black, and wore a becoming gown of dark blue velvet.

"Promise me, Sidonie, that if I send my coach you will visit us next summer." Then, as if sensing Sidonie's hesitation, she added, "If God willing we are still at peace, and all's well with England."

"I will, my lady." Though, thought Sidonie, with a pang of unease, who could say what shadows might lie at the scrying crystal's heart, should she gather courage to look into it?

"Safe journey, Sidonie," said Lady Mary, as she embraced her. "And you, Master Aubrey." With a hint of mischief in her smile she added, "I entrust this young woman to your care — see that this time no harm befalls her."

As the coach moved off, Sidonie looked back and saw Lady Mary in her night-blue gown waving from the arched gateway. Though she knew it was only a trick of light and shadow, Sidonie fancied she glimpsed an elegant, ghostly presence hovering at his sister's side.

ॐ ॐ ॐ

The coach rocked and jolted over the muddy autumn roads, under leaden skies. Though it was a day to dampen the spirits, with a raw drizzle in the air and mist hanging low over the fields, Sidonie was not in the least downcast. Wrapped in a new woollen cloak from the Countess's wardrobe, with a fur rug over her lap and Kit half-dozing at her side, she leaned back at her ease against the velvet cushions. *What strange twists and turns life takes,* she thought. Who could have foretold at the beginning, how this foolhardy adventure of hers would end?

She gazed out the window at shorn grey fields and dripping woods, until eventually sleep overtook her. Dreaming, she revisited the gardens of Wilton House, now mysteriously transformed. Here were undiscovered grottoes, fountains, mazes, walkways, artful arrangements of shape and colour that mirrored in small the grand architecture of the cosmos. And at the gardens' outermost edge, where artifice gave way to Wilderness, stood the Lord of Misrule in motley garb and jester's bells. But his face was not Adrian Gilbert's. This man was thin and harsh-countenanced, and he had the burning eyes of a zealot.

Sidonie woke abruptly as the coach lurched over a rut, and found that she had fallen asleep with her head resting on Kit's shoulder. Discomposed, she drew herself primly upright. Kit smiled and put out a hand to straighten her cap, which had drifted askew. "Look there," he said, turning to the window. "There is Westminster Gate, just ahead. We'll be safe home before nightfall — once again plain Kit and Sidonie, with a deal of explaining to do."

Safe home. But still half caught up in her dream, Sidonie was filled with a terrible unease. She wondered, *After all that has happened, and is still to happen, how can any of us in England think ourselves safe?*

ॐ ॐ ॐ

Sidonie opened the cottage door to a fusty closeness. Clearly, no one had thought to throw back the shutters and air the rooms. Emma, to her credit, had done her best to clean and tidy. The hearth was swept, the floor rushes tolerably fresh, the dishes set out neatly on the cupboard. Still, cobwebs clung to the beams and there was a film of dust on every surface.

"Father!" Sidonie called out. "Father, I have come home!"

There was a clink of glassware, the scrape of a bench pushed back, and Simon Quince emerged from his laboratory, spectacles in hand, wearing a look of surprised delight.

"Sidonie, my child, at long last! How worried I was!" He returned Sidonie's embrace — a little awkwardly, for he was not a demonstrative man; then held her at arms length and looked anxiously into her face. "Are you quite well, my child? When the message came that you were ill, I feared the worst."

Sidonie smiled and kissed his cheek. "Neither pox nor plague, Father, only a fever. I am quite recovered."

"And how fares the Countess? Is Wilton House as splendid as they say? How came Lady Mary to send for you?"

"Mercy, one question at a time! Lady Mary is well, she sends you greetings. Wilton House is surpassingly splendid. And as to the last, it is a long story. But you, Father, you are looking thinner, has Emma not been feeding you?"

"Oh indeed, she has looked after me well enough —
though I must say you have a defter hand with the cooking.
Nay, with the completion of the Great Work so near at
hand, I could not afford to spend much time at table."

"Indeed, Father? You are as close as that to making
gold?"

"One step more, albeit the most delicate part of the
process . . . this time there is no doubt I will succeed."

Sidonie's heart contracted with love and pity. She saw,
as though for the first time, the strands of grey in his hair,
the deep lines that furrowed his brow. His back was not as
straight as it had once been, nor his movements as sure. All
those years of painstaking, futile effort had left their mark.
Suppose that handful of red Glastonbury soil was in truth
the secret elixir? Had she held in her palm the missing
element, the end to all his labours, only to lose it?

What had been found once, could be found again. But
that thought could surely wait for another day.

She took his hand, noticing how stained his fingers
were, how the pads were calloused from decades of using
mortar and pestle. "But if you do not succeed, Father, it is
no matter."

He gazed at her in bewilderment. "How so, daughter?
I promised the Queen on my honour that she should have
gold."

"And so she has. Your promise is kept."

"What mean you, Sidonie? What gold?"

Smiling, she pulled out a bench from the table. "Is that
mutton stew I smell on the fire? I am famished after my
journey. Sit you down, let us eat, and I will tell you of my
adventures. And after that, I needs must have a word with
you on the subject of apprentices."

CHAPTER TWENTY-THREE

Then wilt thou speak of banqueting delights,
of masks and revels . . .
— Thomas Campion, "When Thou Must Home"

The autumn wore on. As she pickled and preserved for winter, sorted apples in the garret, dried the last of the fresh herbs, Sidonie gave little thought to invitations from the Queen. But then November came, and before long it was the seventeenth, when all England celebrated the anniversary of Elizabeth's accession to the throne. Bells rang out across the country, bonfires were lit in every town and village. And still there had been no message from the court.

One December evening when her day's tasks were finished and her father had withdrawn into his library, Sidonie set aside her book and instead unwrapped her scrying crystal. To look into the glass no longer frightened her — she had come to see it as a device, no more — but she could not have explained what odd impulse now drew her to it.

In the heart of the glass there was, as always, a swirl of mist, a captured glint of candlelight. And for some moments, nothing more. Then, just as Sidonie, smiling at her own foolishness, was about to put away the crystal, a blurred image took form: not the letter that she had half-hoped for, but a vessel of some sort, a cauldron or a bowl. And she wondered what there could be about that familiar round-bellied shape that made her throat tighten, gooseflesh rise on her arms, so that she thrust the crystal away in alarm.

ॐ ॐ ॐ

On the afternoon of Christmas Eve Emma rushed into the back garden where Sidonie was cutting holly to decorate the hearth. "Come quickly, Mistress Sidonie, the master has gone out, and there is a fellow at the door, who says he is sent by the Queen."

Startled, Sidonie set down her holly cuttings. "Mercy, Emma!" She had spent all morning cooking, in an old pair of house slippers and her shabbiest gown. She glanced down and saw a large smear of cherry preserves across her apron front. "I am in disarray, go ask him to sit in the parlour while I put myself to rights."

She smoothed her hair as best she could, straightened her cap, put on a clean apron, gave a quick stir to the wheat she was boiling for frumenty. Then, flustered and breathless, she hurried through to the parlour. If the messenger who waited in his scarlet livery was surprised by Sidonie's humble circumstances, his solemn young face gave no sign. With a bow and a flourish, he handed her a letter from the Queen.

As soon as she had seen the messenger out, Sidonie retreated to her bedchamber and shut the door. Her mouth had gone quite dry, and her heart was racing. She broke the royal seal, and unfolded the parchment.

It was an invitation, signed by Lord Burleigh on the Queen's behalf, to the Twelfth Night revels at Greenwich Palace.

She had scarcely time to read as far as Lord Burleigh's signature when Emma shouted up the stairs to announce another visitor. Sidonie folded the letter carefully and put it in her pocket. When she came downstairs and looked out she found Kit by the front walk stamping mud from his boots.

He called out, "The invitation has come, has it not? I met the messenger in the road."

Sidonie nodded. Her heart was still beating hard. "To Twelfth Night at Greenwich, Kit. And you are invited as well."

"What, I?"

"Yes, truly, Kit. Do you come in, I will show you the letter. It is addressed to the both of us." She reminded him, half-teasing, "Have you forgotten we are brother and sister? It would be unseemly to invite one without the other . . . "

"Then for your sake I must keep up the pretence a little longer." Kit finished scraping his boots and stepped over the doorsill. "But sister, have you thought how we are to travel to Greenwich?"

"It is all in the letter. Lord Burleigh will send a boat to fetch us. But Kit . . . " She stopped short and gazed at him in sudden dismay. "The Court at yuletide, the palace revels — everything will be so splendid. What can I wear?"

Kit glanced with amusement at the faded bodice and mended skirt that Sidonie wore for housework. "Perhaps not that," he said, smiling. "But what of the gown that Lady Mary gave you, that you wore home in the coach?"

Sidonie thought about the dress — a heavy mulberry silk embroidered all over in a silver leaf-pattern, with flowing ivory sleeves. Though it was a finer garment than she had ever thought to own, was it grand enough for

Greenwich Palace? Undoubtedly not. But then, what pretensions had Sidonie Quince to grandeur? "I warrant it will do well enough," she said.

"Marry, it will indeed," Kit said, and added gallantly, "I will be as proud to have you on my arm, as if you were wearing cloth of gold."

ॐ ॐ ॐ

When she went to her bedchamber to fetch Lord Burleigh's letter, she saw that she had left the crystal on her writing table. She picked it up, intending to hide it away, then stood with it cradled in her palm, considering. Surely her work was finished now? Or might the Queen still have need of her? She hesitated for a moment, then put the crystal in her purse along with her invitation.

ॐ ॐ ॐ

Another river journey. *Of a sudden, how adventuresome my life has become,* thought Sidonie, as the Queen's boatman rowed them downstream through the still, frosty night. She shivered a little under her heavy cloak, as much from nervousness as from the cold.

When she looked down into the dark water she could see glints and spangles of light from the windows of the great palaces along the northern bank. They glided past the Palace of the Savoy and the Temple. The boatman pointed out the Rose Theatre, newly built across the river in Southwark, though in the early evening darkness they could only guess at where it stood. Perhaps for Sidonie's sake he made no mention of the bear gardens, nor the ill-reputed taverns that lined the southern bank.

Then came the Tower and the grim red walls of Bridewell Prison. Ahead lay London Bridge, so weighted down with shops and houses projecting out over the water, that Sidonie wondered it did not collapse. Just before the bridge at Old Swan Stairs the waterman turned the boat into the bank and bade them alight while he shot through the piers. Too many boats had capsized with all their passengers, he told them, in the torrent of water rushing through the nineteen arches. They went by foot along Thames Street past the bridge to Billingsgate, where the boat was waiting for them at the bottom of the steps.

And there at last on the south bank was Greenwich Palace with all its windows ablaze, overlooking the Thames from a rise of land.

Sidonie clung to Kit's arm as they made their way up the waterstairs and into the glare of torchlight. Kit elbowed his way determinedly through the crowd milling round the palace gates — acquaintances and minor relations of noblemen, many of them in elaborate costume, all hoping to brazen their way past the royal guards, or slip in unnoticed with an invited group.

Opening her silk purse to present her invitation, Sidonie felt something smooth and round. The crystal. In the distractedness of getting ready, and the excitement of the boat journey, she had all but forgotten it was there.

Once indoors, Kit took off his winter cloak to reveal an elegant suit of moss green velvet, with sleeves of claret silk. Sidonie raised her eyebrows in mock reproach. "Fie, Kit, you put me quite to shame, you did not say you would be so modish." Kit blushed. "On loan from my brother, at the Inns of Court," he confessed.

Sidonie observed with faint surprise how handsome Kit looked in his borrowed finery, and with what careless grace he wore his embroidered doublet, its soft woodland green mirroring the colour of his eyes.

Kit smiled, as though reading her thoughts. "'Struth, we are a fine couple, are we not? Come, sweet sister, let us join the revels." And he took her hand to lead her forward.

In the Great Hall of Greenwich Palace there was no end of things to be marvelled at, and she was glad that Kit was there to marvel with her. From the chandeliers hung tassels and fringes of gold foil that shimmered in the light, and everywhere were festoons of ivy, bay and laurel, and bright red clusters of holly berries. The walls were covered with tapestries, and all the gallery rails draped with embroidered cloths.

Because there was to be a masque tonight the vast room with its painted timber ceiling had been transformed into a theatre. There was a gilded stage of splendid artifice, and a scaffolding with rising banks of seats.

Kit and Sidonie wove their way through the chattering, jostling throng. The ladies' gowns were a vivid tapestry of emerald, ruby red and buttercup, topaz and violet and damson. The pervading scent of perfumes and pomanders made Sidonie want to sneeze. What coxcombs the gentlemen were, she decided, in their starched white ruffs, their fashionably slashed and pinked and scissored doublets, their puffed sleeves and padded trunkhose; and the ladies of the court, in their damask and Cathay silk and velvet, their Spanish farthingales and glittering ornaments and ostrich feather fans, made her feel like a milkmaid who had crept in uninvited to the ball.

Presently an usher led Sidonie away to sit with the other
ladies in the seats near the dance floor, at the left hand of
the Queen. It was still two hours before Her Majesty was to
enter the Great Hall and the masque begin.

Seated among strangers, Sidonie turned her attention
to the stage. On the left was a painted landscape of woods
and meadow and near centre stage a pavilion of white
taffeta with marble pillars, lamplit from within. On the
right against a backdrop of battlements rose an ornately
gilded and ornamented castle, with lights shining from its
windows. ("Painted canvas and wooden frames," she could
imagine Kit saying. He was always more interested in the
mechanics of things than in the final effect.) Over all hung
a painted ceiling that was made to look like clouds.

All evening Sidonie had been haunted by a vague sense
of unease. Until now she had put it down to anxiety, to
nervous anticipation. But no, she decided, it was not only
the unfamiliarity of the Court, the splendour of the occasion,
that made her heart beat faster, her stomach knot itself into
a fist. There was a wrongness here. Maybe, she told herself,
it was because this was a night of masks and disguises, of
feasting and tomfoolery, when all things were turned inside
out and topsy-turvy.

And that reminded her of her troubling dream, when
the Lord of Misrule, unmasked, revealed his zealot's face.
There would be no King of Folly elected here tonight. In
King Henry's day the Lord of Misrule had reigned over
palace masques and mummeries just as he nowadays did
in the country villages. But Queen Elizabeth's yuletide
revels were statelier affairs, and her Master of Revels
devised much less boisterous entertainments. All the same,
this was a time of beguilement and deception, when

nothing was as it seemed and ordinary constraints were cast aside. And when so many here were costumed, who knew what elaborate mask might conceal the face of an enemy, what cloth of gold or damask sleeve might hide a dagger meant for the Queen?

She felt for the purse at her waist, ever mindful now of the crystal's presence. What secrets might it reveal on this night of the Epiphany, when things hidden were made manifest?

Suppose it warned of danger — of a threat to the Queen, to England? What then? It was one thing to discover hidden treasure. But to see the future, and yet be helpless to alter it — that thought was more than she could entertain.

And yet her father had argued differently: if a man knew that his house was to catch fire, though the fire was pre-ordained, he still might act on the warning, and save himself.

But now there was an excited stirring in the crowd, and then a sudden hush. Trumpets sounded a fanfare, and all heads turned. First came a procession of court dignitaries — gentlemen, barons, earls, Knights of the Garter — and finally the Queen herself, resplendent in pearl encrusted tawny-orange satin trimmed with lynx skins. Close at her side was the royal dwarf Thomasina, in yellow velvet overlaid with copper gold.

The Queen took her place in her high, canopied seat.

Drums rolled, more trumpets sounded, and the revels began. The torchbearers entered, to the accompaniment of drum and fife, with courtiers and ladies-in-waiting costumed as gods and goddesses and heroes of romance. They glided across the boards in flowing robes of ivory and sea-green and azure, in damask and lawn and taffeta richly embellished with gold and silver lace, in elaborate headresses with sweeping white plumes. Then came the hired actors, the Queen's Men, who took the roles of fauns and nymphs and satyrs, shepherds, clowns and soldiers, ogres and sorceresses.

A courtier in silver and crimson came out to pay extravagant tribute to the Queen, and to explain the meaning of the action. With all the excited conversation in the audience, Sidonie had only the vaguest idea of what he had said, but as the masque unfolded she was caught up in the music, the blaze of light and colour, the clever devices and rapidly changing tableaux.

A live bear emerged from a painted cave and to loud laughter was chased offstage by a comic soldier. An alchemist with a tall, pointed hat, straggling white beard and hair down to his feet stumbled wild-eyed across the stage, mortar in one hand and pestle in the other. He was a figure of absurdity, mocked and taunted by a band of small boys, and Sidonie, distracted for a moment, wondered sadly if this was how the world would come in time to perceive her father.

Clouds parted to reveal the golden dazzle of the sun. The Goddess Athena with spear and helmet descended from the sky, and by means of a hidden trapdoor, Aphrodite rose in white-robed splendour from the foam. Apollo played the panpipes as he and his muslin-draped attendants rumbled and creaked their way across the boards in a flower-garlanded wagon. Then the scene changed to nightfall, and the painted sky above the stage was aglitter with stars. In the intervals there were songs, and verses were declaimed, and the musicians in the gallery played lively airs.

It was as though the players feared this might be their last performance, and they meant to bid farewell with every extravagance of spectacle, every ingenuity of invention.

As the tableaux grew to a close, eight of the Nine Muses — who as Kit would have been quick to point out, were really men — entered in skirts of cloth of silver and embroidered waistcoats, their hair hanging long and loose over cloaks of crimson taffeta. They danced in and out of the white pavilion, presumably seeking their lost sister, and then, moving down from the stage, they invited eight court ladies from the audience to begin the general dancing.

Now there was a murmur of pleasure and a burst of applause as the Queen descended from her seat to join the revels. Light-footed and agile as a girl, she danced a lively galliard. And then one of the actors, a tall black-masked figure in a sorcerer's black robe, bowed low before the Queen, and swept her away into a pavane.

At that moment a shudder of premonition crawled down Sidonie's spine, and the hair prickled along her arms. There was something ominously familiar about that faceless player: something in his way of standing, something perhaps in the stiff-spined, formal way he moved through the figures of the pavane. Behind that velvet mask, the hard knot in her stomach told her, was a gaunt, deep-furrowed face and eyes as cold as stones.

In an agony of indecision Sidonie rose from her place and went to stand at the edge of the dancing floor. Should she cry out a warning? But what if she were mistaken? To shout false accusations at one of the Queen's Men, to bring the dancing to a halt, to have the whole court turn as one with anger and astonishment to stare at her, what then? At best embarrassment, humiliation, the Queen's furious displeasure; at worst — well, she would not dwell on what the worst might be. She drew a long, sobbing breath.

And then the moment had passed. The pavane had ended, the Queen, laughing, returned with her ladies-in-waiting to her seat. The musicians struck up a *volte*, the dancers leaped and stamped themselves to breathlessness, and Sidonie, feeling sick and faint, leaned against a pillar until Kit came and drew her, unwilling, onto the floor.

CHAPTER TWENTY-FOUR

Between the acting of a dreadful thing
And the first motion, all the interim is
Like a phantasma or a hideous dream.
— William Shakespeare, *Julius Caesar*

After the masque and the dancing came the Tournament of Hobby Horses. The riders pranced forth with small neat steps, heads and chests jutting absurdly out of cloth-covered horse-bodies, false legs dangling down in stirrups. For half an hour or so, cheered on by the crowd, they flailed wildly at one another with wooden swords, until at last a winner was declared, and received his prize from the Queen's own hand.

But it was past midnight now, and time for the Queen to lead the way to the Twelfth Night feast. The tables in the long banqueting room were laden with all manner of dulcets, dainties and sugary confections: florentine custards, feathery almond biscuits, jewel-coloured jellies, candied violets, marchpane molded into fantastic gilded shapes. And there was sack and mead, claret and muscadine set out in Florentine decanters.

Kit and Sidonie found themselves at the edge of the crowd that milled round the tables. Sidonie leaned close to Kit so that he could hear above the din of voices. "I feel a little dizzy," she told him. "Nay, do not be troubled," she added, seeing Kit's look of alarm. "It is nothing, only the heat and the excitement. Do you stay here. I will find some quiet corner to sit down."

Before he could protest she slipped out of the banqueting room, retreating into the now-deserted hall. One of the palace guards shot her a quick glance, then, seeming little interested, looked away.

She took refuge in a small wainscotted alcove, half-hidden behind a pillar and a screen. There was nowhere to sit, so she folded her legs beneath her, wide skirts billowing, and set the crystal on the floor. The Queen was in danger. Sidonie could feel it in the prickling of her scalp, the knotting under her ribs; it was like a shrill singing in her ears, a sourness in the air.

She was better practised now, and the vision in the glass came quickly.

There was mist at first, then a gleam of silver. Once again, what emerged was the image of a bowl: no longer blurred but clearly defined, a graceful, curving shape that captured and held her gaze. And as before, the sight of it made her stomach clench, her heart race, so that she knew it for a warning. Remembering that strange night in the Abbey tunnel, she thought, for a fleeting moment, of the Grail. But that was too fanciful a notion. This vessel, she felt oddly certain, was no mystical object, but something earthbound, tangible, a thing of ordinary use.

But there was something else, a second, vaguer image, hovering above the bowl: a thing she had not seen before. She focussed her gaze until gradually it came clear. A bracelet? No, it was smaller than that, and narrower.

A ring. And beneath the ring, a bowl. But then those shapes vanished, and the glass was crowded with scores of masts and bellying sails. They were English ships, the Queen's ships — Sidonie knew that as surely as she knew that she herself was English. But as she watched, stricken, the masts splintered, the proud sails crumpled in the midst of smoke and flame. And then there was nothing to be seen but tentacles of black smoke, and a fierce red glow.

Sidonie wrapped the crystal, put it away in her pocket, and with a sick, empty feeling in her stomach she returned to the banquet room.

Now servants were entering with candles, followed by musicians and trumpeters. Then came various dignitaries of the court, and after them servers and ushers, bearing in triumph the Twelfth Night wassail bowl. The musicians struck up an exuberant tune as the immense green-garlanded vessel, with its heady fragrance of nutmeg, cinnamon and cloves, cider and brandy and roasted apples, was marched round the room and set down steaming on the festive board.

There was still a great crush around the other banquet tables, as courtiers, ladies of the court, invited guests — and a few, Sidonie supposed, who had contrived to slip in uninvited — helped themselves to the rich delicacies. Tonight, it seemed, most rules of protocol were cast aside. Now the players, still in costume, descended on the table: nymphs and shepherds, fairies and fauns and monsters, all intent on snatching up their rightful share.

Some of the Queen's gentlemen had gathered by the high table, and presently they broke into song:

Our cup it is white and the ale it is brown
The cup it is made of the good ashen tree
And so is the malt of the best barley . . .

And it was then, in the midst of that jostling confusion, when all eyes were on the singers, that Sidonie, alert and watchful, saw what no one was meant to see: a hand all but concealed in a drooping black sleeve, lingering for a heartbeat too long above the wassail bowl.

A ring. A bowl.

And Sidonie knew that the moment Queen Elizabeth drank from her glass, England's fate would be decided.

She watched the Chief Steward fill the Queen's cup with a silver ladle, and, bowing, set it before her. No one would drink until the Queen herself, on this contrary night, proposed the toast.

"Drink wassail!" said the Queen. And she raised the goblet to her lips.

Sidonie felt a great cry tearing its way out of her chest. It pierced the babble of voices like a swordthrust, exploded into the hot, crowded room.

"Your Majesty, I pray you, do not drink!"

Startled, the Queen set down her goblet. Her expression was at once furious and disconcerted. Every face in the room had turned toward Sidonie with a look of shocked expectancy.

"Who speaks to me thus?" asked the Queen. Her voice was composed, and icy cold.

All Sidonie could manage now was a hoarse whisper. "Your Majesty, I am Sidonie Quince, the scryer. I have looked into the crystal, and have seen disaster — for you, for England."

Lord Burleigh and several of the court dignitaries had stepped forward, but the Queen waved them back.

"What manner of danger, Sidonie Quince?"

"The wassail bowl, Your Majesty. The danger is in the wassail."

Now it was Sir Francis Walsingham who spoke. Sidonie had not forgotten that stern, sombre face. "You talk of poison, Mistress Quince? Her Majesty's taster has already drunk from the wassail bowl, and suffered no ill effects."

"I fear, sir, that it was done these few minutes past."

"Think carefully what you say, Mistress Quince. Who do you suspect? A servant?"

Someone, a courtier, observed, "The wine is served in Florentine glass. It is well known that Florentine glass will explode if it comes in contact with poison."

"And on the strength of that, would you risk Her Majesty's life?" demanded Walsingham. His tone was scathing.

From the corner of her eye, Sidonie saw the man in the sorcerer's robe sidling quietly towards the door. All uncertainty vanished.

"No servant, Your Majesty. That man." And she pointed.

"Seize him," said the Queen. At once half a dozen court officials has surrounded the man, and held him fast.

"If it please you, sir," said Sidonie, looking at Walsingham. Her legs felt too weak to support her; her mouth was so dry it seemed that her words must surely catch upon her tongue. Kit, standing quietly beside her, took hold of her hand. She gained courage from that firm, warm grasp. "If you would bid him unmask?"

"Do as she says," said the Queen, before Walsingham had a chance to respond.

One of the guards reached out and snatched away the mask. The pale, lank hair, the dour, deep-furrowed face: there was no shade of doubt.

"Sir Francis," she said, "if you would have him stretch forth his hand?"

The assassin stood stone-still and unsubmitting in his captors' grasp. His cold, remorseless gaze was levelled at the Queen.

The guard seized the man roughly by his wrist, lifted his arm, flung back the drooping black sleeve.

A jewelled ring, large and many-faceted, glittered ruby-red in the candlelight.

"Send for an apothecary." Walsingham said.

"If it please you, sir . . . my brother has trained as an apothecary." As Sidonie spoke, she sent a wordless plea in Kit's direction; and Kit — unquestioning, unhesitating — stepped forward. At Walsingham's nod he approached the assassin and examined the ring.

After a moment he looked up. "The crown of the ring is hinged, and underneath is a secret compartment. There are still traces of oil, and a smell of bitter almonds."

The Queen's eyes narrowed; whether or not her face paled, there was no telling, under that smooth egg-white mask.

"Cyanide, then?" said Walsingham.

"I'd stake my life on it," said Kit. Those words, unthinkingly spoken, sent a chill through Sidonie. "And other ingredients, I think. Belladonna, mayhap; hensbane, monkshood, black hellebore. With so potent a mix a few drops could suffice."

"Fill a cup from the bowl," the Queen told one of the servers. "Give it to this man to drink."

There was deathly silence in the room as the server ladled a cupful of the hot brew into a cup. When he held it out to the assassin, the man flinched, and held up one hand as though to refuse it. His face had gone the colour of ashes. Kit, returning to Sidonie's side, gripped her hand hard.

Walsingham had stepped forward, as if about to protest. It would suit him ill, to forfeit the chance of interrogation. But clearly, the Queen would brook no interference by her spymaster.

"Drink," she said, her voice low-pitched and steely.

The man's fingers closed around the cup. For an instant Sidonie thought he meant to dash it to the ground. Then, in one swift, defiant motion he lifted it to his lips, threw back his head, and drank.

Still no one stirred, or spoke. It was as though, for those first waiting moments, time had stopped. Sidonie, watching with held breath, thought, have I accused him for naught? Then, abruptly, the man's hands flew up to his throat. Sidonie could see all the cords standing out in his neck, hear the rasping wheeze of his breath. His face had turned the colour of beetroot. Foam flecked the corners of his mouth.

His knees buckled, and still clutching his throat, he sprawled full-length on the rush-strewn floor. His arms flailed; wrenched by convulsions, his back arched like a bow.

I have made this happen, was Sidonie's first horrified thought. *Is this the revenge I wanted?* And then, shuddering:

was it thus my mother died? She buried her face in Kit's shoulder. His arms went round her and he held her fast.

There was a great, collective sigh, as though everyone in the room — courtiers, guards, servants, the Queen herself, let out their breath at once. Sidonie raised her head and summoned the courage to look. The assassin's body lay motionless. "Take him away," she heard someone — Walsingham? — say. "It's over," Kit said, amid a rising hum of voices.

"How horrible." It was all Sidonie could think to say. "How horrible."

"It was the better choice," Kit said, "and quickly done. More merciful than Walsingham's questioners, and a traitor's execution." All the same, the colour had drained from his cheeks.

But now one of the Queen's ladies was approaching through the crowd. "Mistress Quince, the Queen would speak with you in private."

Sidonie gave Kit an anxious look; then, meekly, she followed the brisk swish-swish of the lady-in-waiting's voluminous skirts.

CHAPTER TWENTY-FIVE

The winds command me away. Our ship is under sail. God grant we may live in His Fear as the enemy have cause to say that God doth fight for Her Majesty as well abroad as at home."

— Letter from Sir Francis Drake to
Sir Francis Walsingham, April 2nd, 1588.

The Queen, with several of her ladies, had withdrawn to a small tapestried, pillow-strewn chamber. Her face, under the bright auburn wig, seemed thinner and older than Sidonie remembered. Seen close-up, through the chalky mask, there were deep lines etched around her mouth and eyes.

"Leave us," said the Queen to her ladies. Then, fondly: "All but you, Thomasina. I have no secrets from you, my poppet."

Thomasina smiled and reached up to pat her mistress's hand. How like a doll she is, thought Sidonie, with her childlike body in its ornate gown, her clever, impudent woman's face.

The Queen turned to Sidonie. "Mistress Quince, it seems that once again I am in your debt."

Sidonie could only think to dip a curtsey.

"Once before you scried for me, but then it was mere pretext. I knew well enough what the glass would show. But now it seems my enemies are everywhere. Do you scry for me now, Mistress Quince, for I will sleep easier, knowing what is in store."

Sidonie felt her stomach clench, her heart begin to race. What had she expected from the Queen? Gifts, gratitude, security for her father? Willing or not, a place at court? But not this. This was greater peril than she had bargained for. Suppose what she saw in the glass was the death of the Queen? Under the law, such a prophecy was treason.

But the Queen was waiting. *If I tax her patience*, Sidonie thought unhappily, *it will only make things worse.*

She found her voice. "Your Majesty, you have bidden me always to speak truth when I look into the crystal. But what if that truth offends you?"

"My child, I have never yet risen in the morning, knowing what the day might bring. Traitors in the palace, assassins in the crowd, Spanish galleons in the Channel . . . It is best to be forewarned."

Once again Sidonie took out the crystal. The Queen sat down in a rustling of pearl-encrusted satin, with Thomasina, eyes wide and attentive, on a cushion at her feet.

In the glass, a swirling, eddying blackness.

"What do you see, Sidonie Quince?"

"Only darkness, your Majesty. Storm clouds, mayhap."

"As one might expect," the Queen said wryly. "Tempest, flood, eclipses of the moon and convulsions of the earth . . . Did you know, Sidonie, that such are the predictions for the coming year?"

"So I have been told, your Majesty."

"Then prithee continue. Darkness, still?"

In the depths of the crystal, shapes emerged. "I see ships, your Majesty. A great multitude of ships, like a black floating wall, abristle with turrets."

"How many ships, Mistress Quince?"

"Too many to count, Majesty. A hundred or more."

"Spanish ships?"

The image was clearer now. Sidonie could make out the Spanish colours snapping in the wind. She glanced round at the Queen. "Yes, your Majesty."

"Nay, do not look away from the glass. Tell me what else you see."

"I see the line of English ships, and the Spanish ships in a great curving half-moon, standing fast against the English guns."

"This does not bode well for England, Sidonie Quince."

"Marry, it does not, your Majesty. But wait . . . now I see ships with fire running up their rigging. Eight tall vessels, all in a line with their sails ablaze, carried by wind and tide towards the Spanish fleet."

"Fireships," said the Queen. "The engineer Giambelli's infernal device. Hellburners, they called them in Antwerp, and they put God's fear into the Spanish. And now?"

Where there had been darkness in the glass, there was suddenly incandescence. Sidonie shielded her eyes against the glare.

"Fountains of sparks shooting up. Flames gusting, billowing. It is as though the sea is on fire."

"That will be the guns exploding," said the Queen. There was as much excitement in her voice as apprehension. "God willing, Master Giambelli's fireships could save the day."

As Sidonie watched, the red-hot furnace-glow faded. There was darkness again, lit up by erratic bursts of flame. Through dense black smoke, Sidonie glimpsed toppled masts and ragged topsails foundering in heavy seas.

And at the last, she saw the great crescent-shaped line of Spanish galleons scattering in disorder before the English fleet.

Sidonie tore her gaze from the crystal, and looked up at the Queen. Her throat was dry, her eyes burned; pain like an iron vice gripped her skull. "By wind and fire and tide, your Majesty. That is my prognostication. By wind and fire and tide will the Spanish be defeated, and England saved."

"And by the will of God," said Queen Elizabeth. And Sidonie, obediently, echoed: "By the will of God." If either voice was lacking in conviction, only Thomasina was there to overhear.

EPILOGUE

Sweet Thames, run softly, till I end my song.
— Edmund Spenser, *Prothalamion*

Blackfriars Theatre, 1612

The tallow candles sputtered, burning low. On Prospero's island Ariel sang, Ferdinand and Miranda were joyfully betrothed and the monstrous Caliban set free. Prospero announced his intention to give up the arts of magic and retire quietly to Milan.

The patrons who had bought expensive seats on the long Blackfriars stage stretched luxuriously to show off their even more extravagant garments. In pit and gallery, the audience stirred from its waking dream, and prepared to go out into the autumn night.

Sidonie lingered on her bench in the twopenny gallery, still lost in the magic of the play. Kit, more practical-minded, had gone to buy fruit and nuts to sustain them on the journey home.

"Mistress Quince, well met!"

Sidonie looked round with a start.

"I trust you have not forgotten me? Though it's half a lifetime since we dined together at Wilton House."

The auburn hair was thinner now and flecked with grey, the high forehead etched with lines. But his was a face one did not easily forget. Sidonie said with astonishment and delight, "It *is* Will of Warwickshire, is it not?"

"One and the same. Though older, and I fear a deal more care-worn. And it *is* Sidonie Quince?"

Sidonie laughed. "Sidonie, still — but Mistress Aubrey now."

"Ah yes, the young man you told us was your foster-brother — a ruse we all saw through at once. And you were the alchemist's daughter — Miranda to your father's Prospero."

"No match, methinks, for your Prospero . . . though he tinkers still with his vials and alembics. Unlike Prospero, he is not wise enough, or content enough, to give over the Great Work and doze in his slippers by the fire."

"And you, Mistress Aubrey? I remember you had more taste for mathematics than for poetry."

"I amuse myself a little, still, with numbers," Sidonie told him.

"I have seen your translations of Hypatia of Alexandria," he said, surprising her.

"But my words do not soar as yours do, Master Shakespeare. I swear, sir, you turn the basest words to gold. And this play tonight, after so many dark works, was a thing of sheer enchantment."

"My best, I think. I will not write another like it. Do you not feel, Mistress Aubrey, that all the magic has gone out of the world?"

"Sometimes," she said. "'Tis true, the world was not so sombre a place when we were young. Yet I'm told that this Tempest was a great success at Kings James's court."

"Aye, and at his daughter's wedding — another Elizabeth. But the likes of our first Elizabeth, our Gloriana, we shall not see again. Who could forget the morning she went by barge to inspect the army at Tilbury, clad all in white velvet, with a silver breastplate like a warrior queen, pearls and diamonds in her hair, and a silver truncheon in her hand? I play with words, Mistress Sidonie, as you play with numbers. But the game Gloriana played was with the fate of nations, and she transmuted that darkest of years into an Age of Gold."

"And that, Master Shakespeare, was alchemy indeed," said Sidonie. She knew he would gladly have kept her there a little longer, sharing memories in the fading light. But here at last was Kit, to take her home.

ॐ ॐ ॐ

EILEEN KERNAGHAN lives in New Westminster, British Columbia. *The Alchemist's Daughter* is her sixth book in the fantasy genre. *The Snow Queen* (Thistledown, 2001) won the Canadian Science Fiction and Fantasy Award, the Aurora, for best long-form work in English, and was short listed by the Canadian Library Association for Best Children's Book of the Year. Her earlier *Grey Isle Trilogy* won a silver medal for original paperback fiction from *The West Coast Review of Books. Songs from the Drowned Lands* won the Canadian Science Fiction and Fantasy Award, while the third book in the series, *The Sarsen Witch,* was short listed for the same award. The experimental *Dance of the Snow Dragon,* a young adult fantasy novel with a Tibetan Buddhist background, was published in 1995 by Thistledown Press.